Drift

By Benjamin Knopke

AmErica House
Baltimore

© 2002 by Benjamin Knopke.

All rights reserved. No part of this book may be reproduced in any form without written permission from the publishers, except by a reviewer who may quote brief passages in a review to be printed in a newspaper or magazine.

First printing

ISBN: 1-59129-619-6
PUBLISHED BY AMERICA HOUSE BOOK PUBLISHERS
www.publishamerica.com
Baltimore

Printed in the United States of America

Part One
Chapter 1

His eyes were sticky and insecure as they followed Johnny Bea's back all the way through the entry hall. When Johnny arrived, he purposely, yet arrogantly, let the front door remain open. He was brazen enough to believe that every door he entered had someone waiting behind to shut it for him after he passed through, if not open it for him in the first notion. This night the door remained open, and as Johnny greeted his obsessively unintelligible group of adorners he turned around after only two handshakes when he failed to hear the clap of the wooden door refitting back into its threshold.

Johnny Bea had inherited nothing from his mother, with the exception of the ability to accommodate those who had been granted obscenely obvious injustices and the temporary affect to romanticize any woman or man he desired. Of course, Johnny was without a doubt the most primal heterosexual person that I had ever met, however, he had an innate ability to captivate those certain few male peers of his not only through his brawn, but more impressively through his intermittent strokes of diffidence. He could turn this attribute off and on seemingly at will, but mostly when he needed to use it for personal enhancement, or gain. And that was even more impressive than the characteristic itself: the fact that he had the deftness to make the even merely disillusioned not know any better. His success rate was well validated; he even had me fooled at first. But after three years of close acquaintance with Johnny Bea I was finally able to decipher, and properly dismiss, his clever dominance wiles, unlike most, especially those synthetic souls that bowed down to him every chance they got. They were hopeless, and helpless, and they played right into Johnny's hands.

A pure street fighter was what Johnny really was. A crude, mean, rugged brawler without an ounce of trepidation in his body, ready to throw down before the hat even dropped if you looked at him off beam. This made up most of his psyche, and this was not gifted from his mother. This was directly passed down through Frederick 'Oswald' Bea: his thick-headed, thick-tempered father who took it upon himself to completely discount his given birth name and reappoint it as 'Oswald' in the winter of Sixty-Three. As conventionally obstinate as humanly possible, and without having to relocate and still having the ironically hypocritical audacity to claim himself an American, Frederick Bea rejoiced when he heard Kennedy was shot, while the rest of the nation mourned. The only comparison I have ever been able to come up with, yet unable of being even remotely close without doing the compared an injustice, is that of a nineteenth century Tory in Great Britain, and they certainly wouldn't have claimed him after 'Oswald' willingly, and happily, switched his appellation to that of the most despised man on the face of the planet, even if they were convinced the act was performed out of thoughtful principle. 'Oswald' was as shrewd as they came, and Johnny never knew any different.

Johnny's mother, Olive, reluctantly left him only three short months after she birthed him; her soulful dedication to her infant son could not overpower her mind's awareness of the already dangerously volatile situation at hand. After Frederick changed his name, she knew it was time to choose a different path before her fate was sealed. She vowed to herself, even though she was pregnant at the time, to leave Frederick the moment she had enough money to cut loose. It only took her two and a half months to earn enough for bus fare to take her back to her family in Thunder Bay, Michigan and leave St. Louis behind forever.

'Oswald' was always piqued by Olive's sudden ability to conjure up enough money to leave him without having to swindle it away from his own pocket. He mused at the notion of selling herself…ignorantly…and since it was easy enough for him to blame his wife's unexpected insurrection on prostitution, he did just that and felt all the better for it. Not as if he would have suffered sleepless nights if he thought the blame should befall his shoulders; he was way too boorish to have a conscience. He quite enjoyed that she was able to do what was demanded of her…provide him with a son…and then so eagerly take to the road. Quite possibly, that was the only source of derived admiration that he could attribute to her. He had a new subservient son to mold, which was what he required, instead of an undeniably insubordinate, less-evolved, female to raise. Obviously, his hands were full with Olive, and he understood she was beyond control, but if she would have dared provide him with a daughter, no doubt 'Oswald' would have strongly considered suicide in favor of the option, out of pride; there was only one way for him to pass on the profoundly asinine ideals he held so strongly (and not have to explain himself every time he turned around), and that was through a son. I presume the world wished he would have had a daughter, and possibly, so did Johnny.

The unpleasant circumstance of having to meet 'Oswald' Bea has never come to pass for me, and although I am thankful for that, I still am curious. Johnny left the comfort of his father's plush home, and discomfort of his father's unyielding hold, and sought refuge in the basement of St. Michaels Church where he boarded for five years. The Jesuits were able to educate him well enough to earn him a scholarship to a brethren University in Denver, as well as having the political pull to get him out of minor delinquencies he had performed and subsequently been apprehended for during those tumultuous teenage years. Although only verified occasionally through a drunken anecdote, I am positive those were the years Johnny Bea developed into a street fighter.

I stood off in the distance, beyond the crowd of drones that gathered around Johnny. I took a pull off of my whiskey bottle and watched Johnny as he turned around to see who it was that had the insensible defiance not to close the door behind him. I had noticed the naïve underclassman earlier in the evening after I rapidly put a halt to a numbingly mundane conversation Jackie Blasé was trying to hold me into. I cut out for the liquor cabinet, and noticed the raven-haired, shadowy figure standing by the coat rack that was three foot removed from the outer edge of the front door. I didn't notice his piercingly emerald eyes until now. He held a pack of cigarettes in one hand and a bottle of Grain Alcohol in the other. He was inexplicably nervous, and I cogitated that he had heard of Johnny Bea's reputation before gathering the inner-fortitude to saunter on over to Chuck Wylie's Saturday evening pub-crawl. No doubt he was still searching, however, for the strength, because his eyes fluttered and strayed as Johnny's caught them. He slowly took a drink from the bottle of Grain Alcohol that dangled at his side, and then he pulled out a cigarette and lit it. Johnny stared at him vigilantly as the emerald-eyed man seemed to lose his will. Johnny watched him all the way off to the smoking den, and then turned back to his welcoming committee.

"It's going to be one hell of a year, Boys…one hell of a year!"

Chapter 2

"I see you've rejected your primordial appearance over the summer, no doubt to compensate for the abundance of it internally…"

Three years ago I would not have gotten away with a friendly jibe like that, there's never any jibing with Johnny at first, but over the years I have earned his respect as a slightly knowledgeable judge of character and personality…with an emphasis on slightly.

Johnny rubbed over the top of his baldhead with his right palm.

"…It's really very becoming." I added, sincerely.

Johnny's stark blond hair had been receding ever since I first met him, and probably long before that. He had finally discovered the most appealing way to conceal it.

Johnny chuckled a bit, not because he thought the remark was humorous, but because it was true. "I thought you would like it. You know, I thought about you the whole time I was dragging the blade across my head."

"Touché."

I set the bottle of whiskey down on the windowsill I was

leaning against. With his true friends, of whom there were only two, his mother and I, Johnny was willing to show affection even if it was gratuitous and obvious. I anticipated the hug that was forthcoming.

It's not like anybody in their right mind would voice an objection, even if they held one on the inside. Johnny was well tested, and his undefeated status spoke for itself. However, in this age of incessant self-indulgence, many a people were out of their mind, indeed in the wrong frame more times than not, and, unfortunately, it would not be unusual for some narrow spirit to hurl a sarcastic remark in the direction of Johnny showing that affection, and consequently, it would not be any more unusual to find that person lying on the floor unconscious ten seconds later.

"Emerson. Come here my boy!" Johnny flung his powerful forearms out in the most delicate way he could fling them and embraced me.

I wrapped my arms around him and then gave him three welcoming pats on the back. We laughed together, and then I said, "I missed you this summer. I still don't understand why you didn't come down to Florida with my family and I. You know how much they get a kick out of you…"

"Right, Emerson, a real kick…a real kick in the ass!"

"No, I'm serious, they enjoy your company…quite frankly. For some reason, that is beyond my realm of comprehension, they believe you have a mystical aura about you, that your above common thought…you've got them hoodwinked I tell you!"

"One of the goals of every man is to pull the blindfold down upon his elders' eyes…and to be successful at it time and time again. You know that."

We laughed together again, and then shared another embrace.

Albert and Isabella Parks were two of the most interesting people I had ever known. A generation removed from industrialism, they were still industrialists at heart but craved to deny the certainty of it and jettison the whole conviction in favor of a more ideological basis of oneself; they claimed to be transcendental, and therefore they tried to minimize the importance of all logical experience in hopes of being enlightened through irrationality or supernaturalism. They were too systematic to succeed, though, but I commend their optimistic efforts. The entire reason they named me Emerson was derived from this perception. They never told me definitively that I was named for the famous nineteenth century author, but when I began to think critically for myself, I concluded that this was the only rational explanation for my label. To this day, I have yet to encounter another human being, man or woman, with the first name the same as mine. Perhaps, this is an indication of how unseasoned I am? I've only been privileged to travel across the continental United States, and quite possibly Emerson's are a dime a dozen over in Europe? A demoralizing thought actually, one that's rather disheartening.

"You know there's a reason for why I chose not to go down to Florida with you and your family." Johnny stated.

"What's that?"

"My street fighting, if you will, has become fairly limiting…if you know what I mean?"

"The fact that most all of your fights seem to last no more than twenty or thirty seconds, with the end result always turning out to be the same?"

"Exactly, it's become too monotonous…"

"Have you ever considered stopping?"

"Oh Emerson, my boy, just like your parents, an idealist…of all people, I would hope that you would be able to understand that you cannot deny a man his true nature, no matter how destructive or disparaging that nature may be."

"Please, forgive me."

"I took up the organized part of my calling…I became a boxer! A street fighter legitimatized, confined by a ring of rope and bound by fists of leather." Johnny grinned as he reflected.

"I've always wondered why they refer to it as a ring…most likely the person who invented the sport had taken one too many left hooks with his guard down…"

Johnny slapped me across the back of my head.

I laughed and continued.

"…But really, you mean you're studying…or training, shall I say…to become a boxer?"

"No, no. I am a boxer."

"Amateur?"

"Professional, old boy…first bout is next Friday night up in Morrison, at the Red Rocks. A well-known promoter from down under named Austin 'The Aussie' Rafter is holding a three-day inaugural event for first-bout professional contenders. The top two performers encore the weekend and the winner will be signed by 'The Aussie' and will fight his number one contender from his homeland in a real-live televised event…probably closed circuit, but that doesn't matter. The winner, of course, becomes a valid challenger as he tries to climb up the ranks."

Johnny was so proud, not just because he accomplished a set goal that he had made for himself, this summer albeit, but more so because he recognized the utter confusion in my face; he derived more pleasure from the impossibly obvious disarray beyond my eyes; that, I can understand why he waited all summer to inform me about this hobby, per se. Even I found myself startled with humor as my reaction reflected in Johnny's.

"This is exactly why I didn't tell you over the phone…this is too good." Johnny grabbed my bottle of whiskey off of the windowsill and took a pull. "…Come on old boy, let's go grab a chair and I'll tell you all about it."

Johnny wrapped his arm around me, and then led us into the family room next to the smoking den. There was no one in the living room, so we were favored the decomposing green-vinyl couch. Eight to ten people hovered in the smoking den, and the door that led to it was open. A thick coat of smoke carrying a robust smell of tobacco hit my face as I sat on the squishy sofa. I could not discern which was more inviting, the couch or the smoke.

Johnny took another drink off of the bottle and then passed it over to me. Another wave of tobacco smoke from the next room tickled my nose and I could not resist lighting up a cigarette of my own. I offered Johnny one and he took it.

"What? You mean to tell me your trainer allows you to smoke?" I said glibly.

"You're pressing your luck, Emerson. Don't think I forgot about your first remark." Johnny rubbed his palm over his baldhead a second time.

"Oh, come now, you appreciate it. That's why you enjoy my company so."

"You're right. Now give me your lighter."

After Johnny handed the lighter back over to me, I took the opportunity to peer around him and into the smoking den. I noticed the figure, previously by the front door, had knocked off about a quarter of his bottle of Grain Alcohol. He looked to be much more relaxed. The drink served as proper dilution of inhibitions; he was staring at Johnny with misplaced fury beneath his emerald eyes.

I rather wished that this character would not act on that hidden fury, but it was transparently evident that he was going to. Come tomorrow morning, regret is not the only feeling that will be niggling him.

"The first day after we let out for summer break, I acted on my need for more contact, but with structure attached. I still have not found anyone who is properly suited to adequately challenge me as a bare-knuckler…heaven knows I try, all the time…but my confidence within these hands, these weapons of flesh…" Johnny held out both of his hands and then clenched them into a fist. His knuckles whitened and displayed thick calluses on all but the first digits. "…need to be validated through sport. I have not engaged in much sport, at least any that I wish to lay memory to."

'Oswald' had forced Johnny to engage in at least one sport. As long as 'Oswald' could claim the roof as his own, Johnny had no say in the matter. Greenly, Johnny chose ice hockey. He was awful at the sport, the worst on the team. This did not settle lightly with 'Oswald', and Johnny found himself on the receiving end of a cracked whip after nearly every game (the only game in which he was spared the flogging thereafter was the game in which he inadvertently kicked in a goal and the referee did not pick up on it). The consummative leather lashing would always be followed by a tongue-lashing: 'You effeminate little son-of-a-bitch…you're no man, you're a disgrace to the species…I should have allowed you to run off with your mother, then you would have been able to harbor your grotesquely feminine qualities. How can my son be so bad at sport? You're a Bea for Christ's sake!' Johnny never really understood what his father was talking about, nor did he care to understand. I would have run away too, only earlier.

Johnny continued, "I had heard about a local trainer from that old poetry professor I had last year…damn required courses…the class in which I understood nothing other than the fact that Mary Case always sat two desks in front of me and to the right...oh what a set of legs...what is that professor's name?"

"Babbage."

"That's it, Babbage...that old coot, I liked him. He knew I was interested in fighting...you know how word gets around campus...and he offered to put me into contact with an old friend of his who just happened to be a boxing trainer, if I was ever inclined to 'elevate my hobby to a level of authenticity'...Hah, Poets, they make me laugh...at first mention, I thought nothing of it, but over the winter break, when everyone was gone for the holidays and I was stuck here, I had time to ponder the thought. It took me three and a half months to fully commit my mind to it. So, the day after Spring Semester let out, old Babbage hooked me up with Percy Leonne, the most honorable French-Canadian you will ever meet...a man of pure principal and integrity. Percy took one look at me and in broken English said, 'Throw on leather...Merci...I want to see you dance on canvas...Merci'" Johnny grinned as he took a drag off of his cigarette. I couldn't help but to find humor in his raw sarcasm as well.

"That was the very first day I met Percy, and I knew right then I was going to be a professional prizefighter. I found my calling Emerson. The entire street fighting phenomenon has just been a precursor to the real vision. I'm going to be the lightest heavyweight to ever win the title, you'll see." Johnny slapped me lightly against the back, but not so light that it didn't cause me to fall forward.

We laughed together again, and then drank together.

"Have you had any fights? I mean, of the amateur nature?"

"Two. Knocked the first one out in thirty-nine seconds, and knocked the second one out in eighty-seven...quite a feat considering they were wearing heavy headgear. After those two decisive bouts, Percy knew it was time to raise it to the next level. We would be wasting our time and energy going through the amateur ranks...of which there really are no ranks...otherwise. Time and energy that would be much better focused on the professional level. I'm in my prime. I have an instinctive ability to fight, a quality Percy has rarely seen, if ever, and he doesn't want to allow it to slip away."

"Don't consider me out of line Johnny, but professional boxing is much different than amateur boxing, and they're both a far stretch from street fighting..." I noticed contempt festooning down upon his tightly drawn face. "I'm just looking out for you, friend."

Johnny slapped me on the back once again, this time much harder. The skin on his face loosened back up. "Much appreciated old boy, but Percy and I know exactly what we're doing. I'm going to rise to the top Emerson, through these face-knockers..." Johnny displayed his fists a second time.

The crew who had greeted Johnny when he originally walked in overheard his excitement. Each one of them screamed in cowardly adulation. The people in the smoking den did the same...all except for the emerald-eyed character; he began walking towards us as Johnny basked in cosmetic glory.

"Does this mean you're going to put your street fighting in the background?"

Johnny laughed hysterically, as I realized the ignorance my question was glazed with.

"Can't deny a man his true nature, old boy...now drink up."

I took the bottle from him and then said, "Good, because your reputation precedes you, and those who wish to challenge you are always looking for an opening."

Johnny settled his outburst as he looked at me with question.

I signaled, with my eyes, to the figure coming up from

behind him.

As Johnny turned around, he felt a bottle graze the back of his blunt head. Blood slowly poured out of a laceration the contact of glass against flesh had made.

This only infuriated Johnny.

The emerald-eyed man found himself face down on the floor after a quick one-two by Johnny. This did not render him unconscious, though, and he struggled to regain his footing as Johnny rubbed the back of his head and inspected the blood.

Johnny pressed his finger against the tip of his tongue to make sure the blood was real. "Now you did it!"

Johnny knocked his opponent back down to the floor and then turned him over. He beat him senseless and bloody with eight straight rights to the chops. He might have beaten him to death if Chuck Wylie and his group of friends didn't restrain Johnny.

I sat and observed the whole incident while smoking my cigarette.

The emerald-eyed man was no longer, as the green iris became but a mere fleck washed out by crimson.

Chapter 3

Jackie Blasé was eternally a Midwesterner and ruefully a bourgeoise, but ever since a family vacation in Seventy-Five to an artificially aristocratic resort in Cape Cod she yearned to be forever linked to the pretensions of wealth and establishment. The thought of tennis on Tuesdays, flummeries on Fridays, and scotch with the Senator on Sundays appealed to every fiber and follicle within that petite frame of hers, so much so that she earned herself a scholastic scholarship to a Catholic school in order to rub elbows with the blue blood of the faith. Unfortunately, her common sense was outmatched by her book sense, and her fragile mind was not aware of the fact that all of the potentials she sought at our quaint institution were Midwesterners themselves who came from new money…Wall Street money…not railway or industrialist money passed through the generations; the potentials she anticipated, and hoped to find, were mainly of the protestant persuasion and wouldn't dare attending a Jesuit college unless it was for athletics, and our athletic programs struggled just to survive affiliation within the conference. No Vanderbilt's found amongst the spires of our humble campus…thankfully.

Much to my dismay, Jackie Blasé was under the impression that I fitted the mold of one of her potentials, and even more to my consternation, she nipped at my ear every chance she got. This was quite a problem, for our campus was rather diminutive, and it would not be out of the ordinary for me to spot Jackie parading through the quadrangle, twirling a lock of auburn hair in her forefingers, seeking out potentials…myself in particular…at least twice a day. On most occasions I was able to avoid her unscrupulous hankerings by way of required refuge behind a trusty old evergreen three times the width of my body.

I didn't much enjoy having to make an effort to avoid Jackie, nor did I enjoy the feeling of having to ignore her in the first place, but her detestable style of finding a suitor, and the perfunctory manner in which she seemed to go about it, was so exasperating that it made my head hurt.

I, of course, was not from the East coast. It's possible Jackie knew this…in fact I rather hoped she would after three years…but at this point her rationale has passed my capability of comprehension…maybe she was just looking for a friend? Or, maybe it was a literal way of trying to live up to one's surname?

The beneficial aspect of being held in the regard in which Jackie held me was that I could use it to my advantage when necessary. I was not self-serving or self-absorbed like Johnny, and I certainly felt guilty after taking advantage of someone's genuineness…even if it was unbearable in its nature…but there were certain moments in life when one found himself in a bind and had to pool his every last resource in order to get out of it. My black, Nineteen Seventy-Seven Thunderbird was rendered stock-still last week after the alternator failed on it. What normally took only a few days, at most, to right the wrong had turned into over a week, and Johnny's first professional bout was tonight. Jackie Blasé had a brand new jet black Cherokee: the new primary choice of transportation for all elitist women…even those in the East…and a trifle thing, which didn't seem so trifle when a favor wasn't needed, such as having to endure Jackie Blasé for a night would not stand in the way of being witness to my only friend merrily throwing his newly legitimized fists around in an authentic environment.

The smell of fresh leather greeted my nose shortly after Jackie opened the door for me. "I'm so excited you invited me to join you on this eventful night. You're such a friend, Em."

After three years, Jackie still had not learned to pronounce all the syllables of my name to keep with its true form. The thought of passing the fight over in lieu of the circumstances quickly shuffled through my mind.

I had to make the best of the situation. I closed the door behind me and the new leather squeaked when I arranged myself in the seat. "I know how much you crave blood, Jackie, especially that which is blue."

"Huh?" She looked over at me quizzically and saw me grinning. As if her memory preferred not to hold onto that thought, immediately she forgot about it and shifted the car into reverse.

Once we hit the interstate, mysteriously, Jackie turned to me and said, "Do you like Rachmaninoff?"

Pleasantly surprised, I turned to her and studied her face. Her bleached white teeth shone through thin lips; either she had done her homework in anticipation of this moment, or she was lying. I reckoned the latter.

Jackie Blasé was not harsh to look at once you got past the personality, but I have yet to encounter anyone capable of surviving the throws of her track. Long, straight auburn hair circled her ashen face as her sapphire eyes added an intriguing twist to her otherwise dull features. The thin lips did nothing, they were placid and flat and creased every half-inch, and her oblong nose was effective at detracting from her captivating eyes on too many occasions. The body that lay support was just as dull...not many curves...with the exception of her hips, which to her credit cajoled men to a second glance when subtly shaken or swaggered. Her feet were disproportionately long for the length of the rest of her body, but her toes were always well manicured, which made the balance of her body not seem so off kilter; tonight they were painted in a sexy burgundy color. I couldn't help but to look twice at them. She wore a pink and white sundress with intricate floral designs on it, and her white (open-toed) sandals matched the outfit accordingly. Her hair glistened in the glow of the sun as we headed toward the mountains. The foothills were only twenty minutes away, and the Red Rocks were only ten after that.

With creeping suspicion, I said, "Actually, I think he's overrated as a composer, but his talent with the ivory is unequaled."

Jackie glanced over at me and smiled.

I pulled out a pack of cigarettes from my shirt pocket and asked, "Do you mind if I smoke?" Normally, I would never have needed, or wanted, Jackie's permission...on anything...but out of respect for the new car, as representative as it may be, I found it polite to ask.

"Sure, Em, just roll down the window...if you will please?"

I searched for the handle to turn the window down, but could not find it.

"Oh, sorry. Here...it's electric." She depressed a button from the console of her door and my window retracted halfway. I looked over at her with a wry grin. She deliberately smiled back. That was intentional.

"So you enjoy Austrian Classic, do you?"

"Very much so."

At that moment, my suspicion of her mendaciousness toward her appreciation of Rachmaninoff was confirmed. "When and where did you first happen to hear any Rachmaninoff?"

"Over the summer, when I was back home in Tulsa, my mother was holding a bruncheon one day…you know not a brunch, but not a luncheon either; a bruncheon…and Lilian Foster, of the Foster food chains, brought out this cassette tape of his music. When she played it, the revelry halted at once. Every woman at that party stopped to listen to his piano playing…momentarily of course, for gabbing takes precedence over music at bruncheons."

I couldn't believe what I had just heard. I would never again derive the same pleasure from listening to Rachmaninoff in the future, as I had previously, before this conversation. Possibly, I might never be able to listen to him again.

"What are you planning to do when you get out of here?" I desperately needed to switch gears, in fear of losing respect for the artist altogether.

"I'm going to reside in Boston, or New York even."

"By yourself?"

"Why? You looking to take me, Em?" She averted her eyes from the road and focused them directly on me.

I couldn't contain myself. She laughed with me to disguise her underlying meaning.

"I don't think so." I replied.

"Oh well, your loss."

Jackie must have forgot about, or ignored any further answer to the question, because she turned back to the road and fell silent while yielding a fastidious grin.

Jackie Blasé was devastatingly annoying, but I couldn't help finding myself curiously aroused by her demeanor in this confined quarter. "No really, who are you going to go to the

East with?"

"Whoever takes me." The same expression remained on her face.

I couldn't help but to smile. "That simple?"

She slowly nodded her head with confidence.

I faced the road and observed the red sun. It was beginning to set behind the peaks of the Rockies.

It was an entrancing evening.

Chapter 4

The twilight provided such unrelenting beauty over the Red Rocks that it became clear where the name originated from. The bleachers...or seating...were better equated to concrete steps, and their grade was steeper than any amphitheater-style seating I had been exposed to. In front lay the stage, just like any other performance arena, wood-planked and brown, but tonight a boxing ring stood atop it. The luminiferous bulbs from above numbered in the hundreds, but only half of them were lit this night; they were focused directly upon the ring. The ring was old and tattered...seen its finer days...but I presume 'The Aussie' spared all expenses to collaborate an unprecedented event like this one; there were no sponsors, no television, no cameras, no advertisements, no frills...just a two hundred dollar entry fee. I had pondered the legality of the event, shortly, before the ride up, but the concern didn't weigh on my head enough to keep me from attending. The event required at least four entrants, but no more than twelve. Nine had entered by way of contest entry fee. As advertised by 'The Aussie' and the local gyms, half of the proceeds would be dispersed to the winner. The only other requirement was that each entrant be in the heavyweight class.

The pamphlet that Jackie and I, along with the other spectators, were provided at the gate revealed each boxer's dimensions, or classifications. Upon scanning the pamphlet, I noticed Johnny was the lightest of the fighters, weighing in at one hundred eighty-two pounds. He was not the shortest, though, for that honor was bequeathed Marty 'The Mauler' McCourt, a two hundred sixty pound, seventy inch Irishman who spared Johnny two inches. The first bout commenced at eight o'clock sharp. Since there were an odd number of entrants, it was unclear as to how they were going to match up the contenders, and the pamphlet had not supplied that information.

The rules were fairly standard and straightforward: the three knockdown rule and the standing eight-count were both in effect. The bell could not save a fighter, and the referee or the corner could stop the fight at their discretion. The rounds were three minutes apiece with a one-minute corner break between; there were twelve rounds in all. I suspected Jackie and I would not be witness to a bout lasting more than six, for almost all of the entrants, of whom were flanking us…going through their preliminary stretches and listening to whispered strategies from their trainer while doing so…appeared to be grotesquely out of shape. Johnny, of course, was one of the two that were in shape.

Johnny was standing off to the right of the stage, away from the rest of the group and audience, smoking a cigarette while rubbing the top of his hairless head over and over again. When he finished his smoke, he jumped up and down a few times and then walked over to his trainer, Percy Leonne.

Johnny wore all red trunks with matching boots. He wore no socks or shirt. He held his pack of cigarettes in his hand, and as he approached Percy, the trainer immediately swiped the smokes away from him. He scolded Johnny in French, but Johnny just laughed it off. I smiled as I witnessed the transaction from afar.

After the few moments of mandatory chiding by Percy were complete, Johnny rolled his neck a few times and then Percy placed both of his hands on Johnny's cheeks. He encouraged his fighter while speaking of tactic as Johnny listened obediently and nodded his head intermittently in precise confirmations. When they were finished, Percy retreated to a clipboard and sat back down on the concrete bleachers. Johnny surveyed the crowd and spotted Jackie and I.

I noticed Jackie had her attention focused on a pair of boxers wearing sweat tops from the same gym. They jumped up and down rapidly and chanted an unrecognizable battle cry. She was enthralled by these two palookas…or frightened out of her wits. The expression on her face suggested the former.

Johnny poked fun at me with a fluttering glance as he smiled widely. He rambled through the sparse crowd and made the journey six rows up to greet us. I stood up to shake his gauze-wrapped hand. I felt Jackie standing up and preparing to do the same. This aggravated me deeply, but Johnny found humor in it. Jackie was walking a fine line and I feared she might try and cross it, or…God forbid…expect me to willingly do so.

"I see the legendary Percy Leonne gave you proper rebuke over the cigarette-sneaking behind the stage bit."

"Exactly…legendary in his own mind. He's just trying to act all professional because of 'The Aussie.' He could care less when we're at the gym."

"Not surprising, all French wear their souls on their sleeves."

"French-Canadian, don't forget." Johnny finished.

The two of us shared a laugh, and then Jackie piped in.

"Johnny, this is so exciting, I've never been to a real live boxing match before..."

"This is more of a contest than just one match, Jackie." Johnny corrected.

"What's the difference? They all look the same on television...speaking of, where are all of the cameras?" Jackie swiveled her head back and forth to try and locate at least one camera. When she couldn't find any, she returned with a look of perplexity.

Johnny and I ignored her.

"How's this work, exactly?" I asked Johnny.

"Since there are nine contestants, Jackson over there..." He pointed out the only other in shape fighter of the lot: a well sculpted, nearly three hundred pound mammoth, with the darkest skin I had ever seen. "...receives an automatic bye to the second round because he has the best amateur record, seventeen wins no losses. 'The Aussie' assigns the bouts based on amateur record. Most of these guys have no more than six or seven fights under their belts, and I am no exception...but not old Jackson, seventeen."

"You've only got two, right?"

"That's why I'm up first. I take on Freddie 'Fingers' Anotelli. He claims to hail from Little Italy in New York, but that's all talk, part of his game, everyone knows he's just a suburbanite from Aurora. He's supposed to be real fast with his fingers, hence the name, but I'm going to whoop him anyways. He's all talk."

Johnny's denigration for Freddie 'Fingers' was not contained within idle word, it was wrapped in pure confidence, and one would be foolish to think otherwise.

"Oh, this is so exciting!" Jackie interjected.

Johnny and I looked at her with contempt.

I spotted a concession stand up on the landing at the top of our aisle of bleachers. I pulled out a ten dollar bill from my wallet and said, "Here Jackie, there's a booth up above that has beer...why don't you go get us a couple?"

Jackie grabbed the money eagerly. "Okay."

She squeezed by Johnny and me on her way to the aisle.

"What time is it?" Johnny asked.

"About eight minutes until you're on."

Before Jackie was out of earshot, Johnny said, "You better make it three."

I shook my head in disbelief as he gave me a friendly right to the jaw. "Don't worry old boy, I'm going to steamroll 'Fingers' and then I'm going to steamroll my opponent in the second tomorrow."

"How does that work, not just tomorrow, but through the rest of the tournament...since 'The Aussie' has an odd number of fighters?"

"No doubt Jackson is going to win his first match tomorrow. 'The Aussie' has already counted on that. Since 'The Aussie' believes Jackson is the best fighter, he thinks Jackson can handle two bouts in one day, which he can, so Jackson's second opponent will be the fighter with the next best record who has made it to the third round. Obviously, this contest is single elimination, and it actually turns out that Jackson fights the same number of bouts as the rest of us; only he has to fight two matches in one day. Depending on how one looks at it, that can be either good or bad for the person who fights Jackson to win the contest on Sunday. Since that person is going to be me, I could care less one way or another, because Jackson's not going to last two rounds with me. I'm going to steamroll him too!" Johnny looked around and assessed the competition before he turned back to me. "These guys are all fluffs my boy, and they will soon bear witness the wrath of Johnny 'The Brawler' Bea."

Johnny picked up on some of the slight bewilderment in my face, as I was still running over the calculations of how the matches evened out through the rounds.

I had finally straightened it all out for myself when he said, "Don't worry Emerson, just watch and enjoy."

Jackie returned with the beers. They were contained in transparent plastic cups. Johnny looked around to check for Percy. He was still studying his clipboard of sheets. Johnny filched one of the beers away from Jackie before she even had a chance to offer it to him. He slammed it down. It only took five seconds for him to knock off all twelve ounces.

"Cheers." He parted as he headed back down toward Percy.

"Good luck." Jackie said.

I looked at her.

Johnny didn't turn around; he just punched his fist in the air.

"This is so exciting." She added as she offered me one of the beers.

I grabbed it from her and sat down. A twinge crept up my spine as I took my first swallow. I hoped the alcohol would dull it enough for me to temporarily forget about the cause.

Percy led Johnny to their assigned corner. Freddie 'Fingers' had been in his corner for five minutes prior to Johnny's arrival. The ring announcer used nothing but his deep voice to present the fighters: he was a tall and thin man with a burlap face as rough as his voice. "In the red corner, wearing red trunks we have Johnny 'The Brawler' Bea. Weighing in at one hundred eighty-two pounds, 'The Brawler' comes to us from St. Louis, and is currently a student at one of our local universities. He stands seventy-two inches in height, and this is his first professional bout. His amateur record consists of two wins and no losses. Good luck 'Brawler.'"

Johnny nodded and then rubbed both of his red-leathered fists over top his head simultaneously. I noticed him wink at somebody in the wings, beyond the table of judges that obstructed my view. I strained to view this person, but to no avail, for the judges' panel formed too much of a barrier.

"In the blue corner, we have Freddie 'Fingers' Anotelli. Weighing in at two hundred pounds even, 'Fingers' hails from Little Italy in New York?" The ring announcer picked his eyes up from the fighters' card and looked over at 'Fingers.' An inaudible laugh displayed his disbelief in Freddie's origin. He continued, " 'Fingers' stands seventy-four inches tall, and this is his first professional bout. His amateur record consists of five wins and no losses. Good luck 'Fingers.'" The ring announcer stuffed the fighters' card back in his shirt pocket and exited the ring.

'Fingers' paraded around the ring once for the crowd, which was received with broken applause, and then taunted Johnny with a flurried display of one-twos. The crowd better received this, and the applause increased dramatically. There were even some sporadic whistles and hollers thrown in out of compulsory measure. The crowd was ready to see some fighting.

The referee signaled Johnny and 'Fingers' to the middle of the ring where he explained the rules to the boxers. When they touched gloves 'Fingers' was still taunting Johnny. All Johnny displayed was stoicism, but behind that impassive gaze lurked sudden fury, and I sensed the fight was going to be over before 'Fingers' even had an opportunity to realize it had begun. I had seen that look in Johnny's eyes before. If 'Fingers' had known what was forthcoming, he would have properly removed himself from the ring and defaulted the match by reason of future health considerations. But 'Fingers' did not know what was forthcoming, only I did. I stood up from my seated position in anticipation of the bell and concurrent knockout of Freddie 'Fingers.'

Johnny winked to the person behind the judges a second time as my curiosity almost overtook my interest to watch the 'Fingers' debacle. But, I stood my ground and kept my eyes focused on Johnny.

The bell rang and the two fighters eagerly pushed away from their corners. 'Fingers' tried to land a left jab as soon as he was within reach of Johnny. Instinctively, Johnny bobbed down to his right, and in the same motion exploded with a right hook that connected flush against 'Fingers' jaw.

'Fingers' mouthpiece soared out of his mouth as his upper-body didn't have time to wait for his knees to give out from underneath him. Only the whites of his eyes were apparent as his head bounced viciously off of the outdated mat.

The referee was just as shocked as the crowd; he stood motionless as an ominous silence fell over the Red Rocks. Johnny and I were the only two not surprised by what just occurred.

In the eerie calm of the moonlight, and in the raw reality of what 'Fingers' had just suffered, my unremitting applause was the trigger that returned the facility to normal.

At first, no one clapped, then a unanimous uproar from the audience…with the exception of 'Fingers' entourage.

Johnny smiled in blissful satisfaction and conceited pride, as he ambled back to his corner. Before he could reach it, though, Percy managed to squeeze through the ring-ropes and greet him with open arms. Percy was just as astonished as everybody else, only he was able to rejoice in the comfort of knowing Johnny was his fighter, whereas the crowd was unable to affix themselves in the same manner; they rejoiced in the awe of the total and absolute power that had just been displayed. As Percy's eyes widened…similar to those of a fawn caught in streaming headlights…I could sense visions of fame and fortune running through his head. He embraced his treasure, tightly, and reinforced the fact that Johnny was his find and nobody else's. After they disbanded, Johnny motioned up to me with his right hand (still bound by red leather); the same one that just delivered the blow that will be permanently engrained in 'Fingers' mind and jaw. I signaled back to him with obsequious gestures and grimaces. Jackie sat still, with both of her hands covering her agape mouth. Her eyes showed that although she was overcome with utter amazement she enjoyed what she had just witnessed so thoroughly that the resulting sensuality she derived from the moment alarmed her deeply. As if the life was just ripped out of him, Freddie 'Fingers' Anotelli lay motionlessly on the mat. His trainer snapped his fingers over Freddie's face hastily as he tried to awaken his conscious. The referee sought the assistance of a doctor by way of 'The Aussie' who was standing in front of the judges' panel at the edge of the ring with a look of unmitigated concern…not for 'Fingers' but for himself. Before seeking the doctor, who might only be in attendance by process of pamphlet dispersion (the bottom of the event brochure read: Ring Doctor, Harry J. Crawson, M.D.), 'The Aussie' found it necessary to argue with the referee, and the validity of his opinion, on the seriousness of the boxer's condition.

That of the crowds countered the sigh of relief ejected from 'The Aussie's' lungs when 'Fingers' regained his senses after three minutes. He rose, shakily, to his feet as the referee looked 'The Aussie' off and returned to the middle of the ring to display the winner.

The referee held Johnny's left hand in the air as the ring announcer said, "By way of knockout, only thirteen seconds into round one, your winner is Johnny 'The Brawler' Bea."

After the announcer concluded, 'Fingers' went to hug Johnny in a gesture of sportsmanship. Johnny wasn't buying. With impudence, and loud enough for the crowd…but more importantly the rest of the fighters…to hear, Johnny stated, "Next time you'll think twice about taunting your opponent, especially one of my prowess, you son-of-a-bitch! You're lucky I didn't try to kill you."

I'm not sure what stunned the crowd more, that statement or the right hook.

Percy wrapped Johnny up and constrained him, as his fighter's fury seemed to return; even in the hindsight of 'Fingers' derision and consequent knockout, Johnny still fumed with hatred. 'Fingers' was wise to rapidly retreat out of the ring under the supervision of his trainer.

When Johnny calmed, he returned to his corner with Percy and the two exited between the ring-ropes. The crowd and the other fighters stared incredulously out of impossible admiration. I saw even Jackson took notice, and hard.

As the ring announcer began to announce the next fight, and as the crowd regained their sense of awareness, Percy placed a towel around Johnny's shoulders and then went off to smoke one of the cigarettes out of the pack he swiped away from Johnny earlier.

"Come on Jackie, let's go down and see him."

As Jackie and I walked down the aisle, I noticed the most striking woman I had ever laid eyes on appear from beyond the judges' panel. And, as if lightning bolts were hurled repeatedly at my feet forcing me to stop, warning me that if I wish to proceed I better take the utmost caution and care, I stood helplessly on one of the concrete steps. Her immensurable exquisiteness catapulted my emotions into a world never before exposed, or even imagined. My pores were imbibed with lust.

"What? What is it? Why did you stop?" Jackie asked as she placed her arm around me.

I could pay no mind to Jackie, for this beauty had ravished

my tongue and rendered me speechless.

She seemed to float through the air as she sought her intended destination. My heart dropped to my feet like a lead zeppelin through the clear sky as her lips caressed those of another…Johnny.

Chapter 5

The vision that beheld my heart while I was immobile on the concrete step, and then so assiduously twisted it in the blink of an eye with the subtle union of her and Johnny's lips, now stood before me.

I didn't even know her name; I had only been witness to her extravagant guise for sixty seconds, but the truth lie behind her eyes, and I brooded over thoughts of an eternally shallow soul if I did not have her by my side. Becoming a boxer over the summer wasn't the only thing Johnny had kept from me.

"Emerson, my boy, this is the other reason I wanted to talk to you in person instead of over the phone this summer. Allow me to present Ella Waldron." He hurled his left arm around her as if she was his object to display proudly…some meaningless trophy.

She gladly accepted the role, outwardly, as she mocked a curtsy to me and then held out her hand and offered it to Jackie. Her fingers were slim and delicate and smooth, and they adorned manicured fingernails, not in the gaudy form but in the classy form, suggesting affluence without the pretense.

Jackie took hold of her hand.

"This is Jackie Blasé." Johnny added.

"Exciting name. It's not self-appointed is it?" Ella said. Her sarcasm bit with underlying significance. She summed Jackie up with one touch of the flesh, and she was right on. Her confidence allowed her to get away with such a remark, and actually make it look apposite.

Johnny and I looked at one another with concealed humor. I wondered if my blue eyes had turned green with envy during the exchange.

"Oh go on." Jackie responded with a playful slap to Ella's arm.

"It's a pleasure to meet both of you." She directed her eyes away from Jackie and pressed them against mine. Mutual affinity was present as she paused momentarily to size me up accordingly.

There was an extremely uncomfortable, yet uncontrollable, display of grins between Ella and me; I bit my tongue to distract myself from getting lost in her magnificent curls: the swirling tresses had a silver sheen to them and they made me think of the sun reappearing in the horizon after a black and foreboding storm. She was mysterious yet hopeful and optimistic.

"You met Johnny over the summer?" I needed to say something to avoid her hypnotic attractiveness. However, I wish I had chosen a different question.

Johnny smiled and answered for her. His insolence knew no bounds. "Sure did Emerson. We met in the hallway of my apartment complex."

"Yeah, it was so funny. I had just moved into town and I was trying to move my stuff into the new apartment...I presume you know where Johnny lives, so I don't need to tell you that it's pretty secure...when I found that I had no way of getting into the gate that leads to the parking garage. You need to have a code to get in. I didn't have a code, and for some odd reason there was nobody in the manager's office…out to lunch I rationalized…so I parked my car and all of my belongings in a Blue space out in front of the complex and decided to see if I could find a way inside…"

Johnny's apartment complex, The Montebello, was a decent place to reside, which claimed high security, but in reality was really quite lax. As a matter of fact, one didn't even need a code to get into the gate that supposedly barricaded the outside world from the parking lot and all of its entrances; all one needed to do was push any four buttons on the number keypad and it would open up. The Montebello was not self-contained, and each apartment was accessed by way of outside stairwell or hallway; the dwellings were more like inexpensive carriage houses than moderate apartments.

"…All I had to do was scale the concrete wall that surrounded the pool area. After that, I sought out my apartment number. When I found the correct one, I was presented with another obstacle, for a lockbox was on the door…"

"Damn Montebello." Johnny interjected.

"And just as I was getting ready to give up…that's when Johnny came swaggering down the corridor."

"To the rescue." Johnny brought her in closer to him with satisfaction.

Jackie laughed sincerely but mine was filled with antipathy. Even though Johnny has had a tough past (and if anybody deserved to have things start falling in his favor it was him) I still felt like he didn't deserve this stroke of luck…but he did.

"He offered me nothing but gentleman hospitality until I was able to get everything squared away." Ella concluded. The two looked at one another and smiled.

"Don't forget about the Blue space you parked in." Johnny reminded, purposefully wanting to elevate his smugness even higher.

"Oh yeah, I learned real quick that the Parking Patrol of downtown Denver actually do their jobs…I got a ten dollar parking ticket for occupying that restricted space."

"Which I willingly paid for." Johnny said.

"I told you that it was not necessary for you to do that…but you insisted."

"I know…I wanted to do that for you. You were new to town, unfamiliar with the way things worked at The Montebello, and not to mention beautiful…I would have been a fool not to try and win your heart with chivalry; this bald head, these coarse hands, and this tight face can only get me so far." He was good, I credited him that. His ability to abandon his vanity at critical moments was one of those gifts passed from his mother.

"That's for sure. Initially, I was scared of you." Ella responded glibly as she slapped him against his bare chest. "But that was easy to get over." She added as she proceeded to rub over his pectoral muscles.

The two laughed. Jackie laughed. I realized my first impression might have been off…maybe. Usually, I am such a good judge of character. I was relieved, though, that I might have made a mistake on this one, because up front…outwardly…Ella personified my dream girl.

She batted her long lashes at Johnny. "No, but seriously, I think it was the parking ticket that sealed it for you Johnny."

His restrained grin was fraught with sarcasm. "Are you sure?"

I didn't know what to think, or feel. I looked over at Jackie, not remembering my head instructing my body to do so. She was admiring the empathy the two held for one another. I closed my eyes in uncertainty, as the world seemed to stop while I spun around it. Then, the bell for the next bout rang and snapped me back to reality.

"Come on, let's get out of here and grab a drink." I suggested to the group.

"Great idea." Ella added. She stared at me long and hard...again.

"Definitely." Johnny contributed.

"Okay." Jackie finished. She always seemed to be the last to catch up.

"I've got to go talk to Percy before I leave, but since you and Jackie drove together, why don't Ella and I meet you at The Hill across from campus?"

"Sounds good." I said.

Jackie nodded her head and removed her keys from her purse.

"Ella and I will see you two, at The Hill, in about a half an hour." Johnny finished. He grabbed Ella's hand and the two glided over to Percy. An enveloping charm accompanied them as they walked.

Never before had I thought of Johnny in a delusively alluring fashion. I didn't think he was capable of such a ruse because he is so crass and abrupt, even when he does apply that one enticing attribute...until now. A nasty glint struck my eye, for I could literally feel it. I turned to Jackie and said, "Let's go."

The Hill was host to mainly local patrons, which consisted of the dregs of central Denver. The establishment was not all that convivial, however, when it came to those who attended the neighboring university across the street...especially if you weren't twenty-one. Jane, the co-owner and consummate barkeep, was an ex-cop and she saw to it that no underclassman would be allowed to even make change if they didn't have a valid verification of age. If one of them were propitious enough to slip past her vigilant eye, then they no doubt would be subjected to the gluttonous sponsors that congregated at the bar from open to close, not having a shred of care for themselves, much less anybody else, and undeniably much less any underage, haughty, college student coming for the sole reason of enhanced mockery while sipping on stale beer or watered down scotch. Jane had built the tavern's reputation up over the years that college students were not welcomed, much less invited, and her loyal following of regulars enforced the policy.

Johnny was able to circumvent this, however, by way of literally cracking the skulls of three of Jane's biggest, meanest lushes; he earned himself, and any of his friends, permanent admission into the bar without any question. I was Jane's favorite, but she respected Johnny more.

The exterior of The Hill was in shambles; it struggled to stand two-story and boasted three broken windows on the second floor (I had never been on the second floor of The Hill, nor did I have any desire to go up there, but it was not hard to figure out what went on up there when the expressions on the faces of the locals changed so drastically from ascension up the stairs to descent back down). The awning that covered the walkway to the entrance was Jane's way of thumbing The Hill's nose at everybody who didn't approve of her enterprise...in particular, the university and its attendees. The awning was the only extravagant thing about The Hill. It was all red with no noticeable blemishes. In crisp white letters it read: The Hill-a fine establishment.

Appreciating the irony, I smiled as Jackie and I walked under the awning.

About twenty minutes later, Johnny and Ella entered through the heavy oak door. All the concerns of the world...any concerns...had respectfully avoided them; two separate people, male and female, unified by one purpose:

sought happiness, or better yet, sought love.

I knew Johnny as if he was an older brother though, and I also knew his hoaxes. He was clever when it came to romance. He used a slick tongue to voice his cunning speech in order to achieve his desires.

It should be noted that Johnny is not a hollow man...quite the contrary. His soul is full of character and integrity. He is a man who knows what he wants and knows how to get it. That's more than can be said for most of us who walk around aimlessly in search of something greater, never realizing that the journey is what really matters and not the intentionally unachievable goal.

There are certain times throughout Johnny's life where his extreme pride within himself was advantageous, and tonight proved to be two perfect examples: The boxing match, if it can be called that, and the illustrated infatuation Ella displayed towards him. Johnny deserved every good fortune that came his way, but he didn't have the right to use these gifts (primarily Ella) as if they were some convenient handkerchief...always there when one needs it, knows its role without compromise, and is dutiful in its function; but, once it gets to mucked up, then it comes time to search out a fresh, clean spot, a part never before used; once to this point, the handkerchief's functional allure has lost its versatility, and it becomes a struggle for its companion, and that's when it's easier to discard it and go find another one.

I know Johnny.

Jackie and I had chosen a brown, vinyl-covered booth in favor of a table with barstools. Comfort was what we sought. For a Friday night, even The Hill was not popping; it never popped, but usually it had a fizzle on the weekends. The four circular tabletops with their four adorning barstools, respectively, that occupied the space between our booth and the bar were more filler than anything, because even if the bar were fizzling, these places would be unused, or underused. There was no justification for having them there. I had always found this intriguing. The Hill was one of those places that seemingly operated on efficiency over everything else. The establishment's owners, Jane and her dwarf brother (who looked and acted like he was part of a traveling circus), pinched their pennies so tightly that they diluted the liquor, served outdated beer, and offered sweet pleasantries upstairs. The only reason The Hill was in business was because the majority of the customers were dry drunks or born drunks, neither of which cared if the alcohol was watered down; their senses were so numb and dull that Jane could serve them pure alcohol mixed with cayenne and it would still slide down their throats with the greatest of ease like it was water. So why not skimp a little on the liquor…who's going to care?

I always chose vodka on the rocks when drinking at The Hill. Usually when drinking vodka I would mix it with water (to help take the sting out of it) and ice, but since the water part was already taken care of for me, I ordered the drink absent the water here. I figured it was the most economic way to order at The Hill, and I didn't have to sacrifice the appealing taste of the drink. Jackie ordered the same drink, which I took as a compliment at first, but when we sat down across from one another in the booth it annoyed me. I felt like she didn't deserve it because she didn't understand the logic that went into reaching the decision to order that exact drink. She didn't appreciate it.

I had smoked one cigarette after another, hoping to keep the conversation to a minimum with Jackie as we waited for Johnny and Ella to arrive. Now they were here, and much to my chagrin I realized that my annoyance did not lie, nor end, with Jackie.

Johnny had prudently changed his attire from his boxing trunks to a white short-sleeved shirt and blue jeans. He still wore the same red boxing boots, though. On occasion, Johnny would enter The Hill shirtless, and every time he would encounter trouble. I was pleased to see that civility took precedence over virile bravura at The Hill on this eve…at least for the time being. I had already witnessed one destruction of foolish gallantry by Johnny tonight, which I must say was deeply enjoyable, but one was all I felt inclined to witness today (not to mention, when you authenticate street fighting, surround the pugilists with ropes and rules and referees, there's something sporty about it, which makes it so much more tolerable to eye than watching Johnny lambaste some drunken warrior's soul after he had already obliterated his face with a right jab).
   Ella's gait was subtle yet purposeful, even with a man around her arm. Her quick flick of the wrist in my direction sent my heart fluttering with wonder and curiosity. She had bound her long curls in a rubber band and pulled them behind in a ponytail. Her face was petite and strong, with a jawbone that squared the skin appropriately. A button nose gave her a sense of cuteness and naivety, while dark eyes allured the hopeless man's impure thoughts. Her shoulders were slight but adequately supported her slender neck. Surreptitiously, an oversize cable-knit sweater…leaving her lower form to be accentuated…concealed the form of her bosom. Her legs were long and slender, not muscular, but sleek; this was obvious even beyond the faded denim that covered them. Brown leather cowboy boots added three inches to her height, which equaled her out with Johnny.
   Before they sat down, they motioned to Jackie and I that they were going to the bar to order a drink. I raised my glass to properly prompt Johnny to order me another. He nodded his

head in confirmation.

The bar was only ten to twelve foot from where we were sitting and I could overhear the conversation between Jane and the couple. "It's been a while since we've seen you Johnny, where have you been?"

"Up to no good!" One of the local drunkards from the corner of the bar slurred Johnny's way.

Johnny knew him, and before returning to Jane he nodded, courteously, in the elderly man's direction.

Ella kissed him faintly on the cheek and said, "I've got my hands full with this one…"

"Good for you Darlin.' It's about time someone straighten this one up…that friend of his, Emerson over there, only encourages his machismo."

I smiled as Jane looked over at me. I noticed Ella lean forward to look around Johnny. Her eyes focused on me.

"What can I say, rash and impulse are not becoming of me…I need vicarious means to harbor those two outstanding qualities."

Ella laughed as she read my sarcasm perfectly.

Johnny looked back at Jane, who was smiling, then he looked back at me and said, "Are you sure that you want another drink? Then be good!"

I laughed and then pulled a cigarette out and lit it.

Johnny continued, "I've also taken on boxing Jane. I just had my first bout about an hour ago up at the Rocks."

"Well I'll be…Johnny's trying to go legit…don't you know you can't deny a man his true nature?"

The last comment sparked Ella's curiosity. She awaited an answer from Johnny but was not privileged one. He noticed her out of the corner of his eye. Johnny wasn't trying to hide what he was to Ella, but I don't believe he was prepared to allow her all the goods on him…just yet. Even though they had been together presumably most of the summer, that was Johnny's off-season, especially if preoccupied with a raven-haired goddess; his true colors only shined when he was in full effect, and that mode was unquestionably turned on at the beginning of each Fall, with the start of a new semester, and the prospect of a new crop who wished to dethrone him. Thankfully, for the truly unenlightened, this was Johnny's first semester of his final two.

Johnny smiled effectually at Jane and she obediently averted her eyes. Barkeeps have loose tongues, and Johnny knew this, he was just thrown off a little.

"What'll it be Johnny boy?" Jane asked accordingly.

"Two vodka on the rocks…"

I had explained my drink theory to Johnny; he overrated it and applied it every time he came into The Hill…at least when I was accompanying him.

"And for the lady?"

"Jack Daniels, straight up." Ella answered. This inspired interested eyes, not only from Jane, Johnny, and myself, but even Jackie as well. Ella just responded with a smile as she watched Jane off to the liquor bottles.

When Jane returned with the drinks, two inbred looking, rambunctious, half-cocked, sorry excuses for men stumbled through the door.

"Two double whiskeys Jane." The one on the left yelled.

"Make it four." The other one corrected.

"Oh hell." Jane said with disgust underneath her breath.

Johnny looked at her.

"We've acquired a few more regulars over the summer." She said to Johnny with lowered eyes.

Johnny closely watched the two as they swaggered down to the middle of the bar; they were yet to notice him or Ella.

"Coming right up!" Jane retreated back to the liquor and

poured four highballs halfway full of whiskey. When she handed the two their drinks, they finally surveyed the meager crowd.

They dropped their jaws when they observed Ella. One leaned over to the other and said, "We don't get hussies like that in here too often…what do you think Charlie, I got a chance?"

The man stroked his dirty beard as the other one responded. "What do you mean Clifton, of course you got a chance. I don't see her with a man…all I see is a cue ball sittin' on top of a mountain. That ain't nothing."

Ella's hand instantly clenched Johnny's arm, tightly, hoping to refrain Johnny from responding. "Why don't you two go back underneath the rock you crawled out from? That is, if you're capable of finding your way back, which I doubt." She said.

The two men laughed obnoxiously and mocked Ella.

Ella turned to Johnny and kissed him long and hard, successfully detracting Johnny's attention from the two…momentarily. Johnny grabbed our drinks off of the bar.

"You'll be doing that to me later on tonight, hussy." The one called Charlie said.

"To both of us." His friend Clifton added.

Their detestable laughs returned as they finally found their drinks and started swallowing them.

"Don't pay any mind to them Johnny, they got nothing on you." Ella said as she kissed him again. She meant to be affectionate, not literal. Then, the couple found their spaces in the booth across from one another. Ella sat next to me, and Johnny sat next to Jackie.

"I'd say." I added as Johnny smiled and stared at the two men.

Jackie was frightened senseless, but greenly she was more

scared for us than the two men. She had only been witness to Johnny's boxing, never his street fighting. She was unaware of his capability.

"Don't worry Jackie..." I said as I tried to calm her. "Ella's right Johnny, they got nothing on you...you've already disfigured one man's jaw tonight..."

"That number will be three if those guys say another word." Johnny interrupted.

I turned around to look at the two men. They seemed to have forgotten about Ella and Johnny. "They're harmless, just a couple of drunks running off at the mouth. Don't worry about them...look, if they try anything, I'll stand in. They should get a kick out of that." I tried to inject some humor to relax Johnny's infuriated nerves.

I was not a fighter, I was a lover. Which is a convincing way of reminding myself that I have no desire to throw punches, nor do I have the desire to find if I have the courage to throw those punches; it's much easier to satirize such a notion. This is not to say, though, that I would sit idly by in the face of danger...I would just run.

Johnny laughed with the rest of the table, and then shot one last look over to the two before he refocused.

Chapter 6

"When I was little, maybe five or so, my whole family traveled south to Louisiana…Shreveport to be exact, which is where my mother is from…to attend the wedding of my grandmother's only nephew, my mother's only cousin, Arthur and his fair maiden Abigail…"

I was four drinks deep, while the others were still trailing me one. Everybody's tongues had been slipping for the past thirty minutes or so as the conscious inhibitions of each individual were slackened. Ella had just finished summarizing her childhood growing up in Detroit, and now she was on to one of her most impressionable memories. I was most daunted with her ability to assimilate herself within the confines of a select group…meaning Johnny and I…and make it seem as she belonged all along…been part of it since its inception.

"…As pure as the driven snow, Abigail, as all southern women are…just ask my mother!"

Her wit commanded attention, for it impinged on the eardrum without pity or remorse, bearing over all regard for decency and subjective view in favor of the blunt fact. I took another drink to keep myself from doing, or saying, something foolish and regretful. She gave me another one of her looks, which my subconscious had been importuning her to cease since our introduction, but which my heart had insisted continue. This was a battle my heart was going to win every time.

"Don't get me wrong, southern men are pretty eccentric too, but their eccentricity is mainly limited to the bottle and meaningless liaisons with their secretaries or with high priced call girls. The Southern Belles, if you will, are all over the board: alcoholics, adulteresses, mistresses, prescription drug addicts, non-prescription drug addicts, bulimia, anorexia, schizophrenia, plastic surgery, liposuction, etcetera, etcetera, etcetera...and that's just the stuff they admit. Think their closets aren't full? Think again. Why do you think all southern women love big, open, walk-in closets? That's right, so there's enough room to keep all the baggage hidden!"

Johnny and I joined Ella as she got a kick out of listening to her own brand of humor. Jackie laughed, out of obligation, in fear that she would look silly. Unfortunately, she didn't realize that type of laugh made her look sillier than keeping quiet.

"At least the men down South don't try and kid themselves, or anybody else. If they want to cheat on their wife they don't try to convince themselves of some underlying moral breakdown, or dilemma, and strike a deal with God...bargain their conscience away. They want to have sex with another woman, that's it!" She completed.

"I'm not familiar with the South, or the Southern Way. I'm familiar with Florida, for I've been there on vacation many times, but I don't consider Florida to be a proper reflection of the South; there are too many transients. I bet it would be safe to say many true southerners don't consider Florida to be part of them." I added.

"You know you're right Emerson, when I think of the South

I think of Mississippi, Alabama, Georgia, Louisiana, and South Carolina…and that's about it. Did I miss any?" Johnny finished his question by leaning forward and pecking Ella on the lips.

"No, I think you covered it Johnny. I would have to agree with both of you." Ella responded.

"What about North Carolina? Wouldn't that state be considered part of the South?" Jackie wondered.

Her voice had become exasperatingly nasal and had raised an octave from the effect of the alcohol. Her question, albeit amplified in an annoying manner, wasn't as dim as I had anticipated when I noticed her itching to contribute to the conversation.

"I actually consider North Carolina an enigma, not quite a southern state and not quite an eastern state." Ella answered.

"That's exactly how I characterize it." I added, pathetically. I looked across at Johnny to get his reaction, but he was busy staring into Ella's eyes. He had a grin on his face, but he was not exposing his teeth. I could sense he had that feeling. Ella sensed it to, and she got even further off track.

"What about the wedding Ella? Arthur and Abigail?"

She snapped her attention to me, and Johnny found humor in his ability to entrance her like he did. He laughed childishly.

Ella pulled her bunched locks out from the rubber band that held them together, and then refitted the ponytail. This was the sexiest gesture she had made all night. She smiled at me and said, "Oh yes, the wedding…I do believe these whiskey drinks are starting to get to me…"

"Me to." Johnny added in a sensual voice.

Ella glanced back over at him. She was noticeably aroused. I could tell even Jackie picked up on the sexual innuendo. Jackie smiled and fluttered her eyelashes at me. I feared I might be drunk enough to make a thoughtless mistake later on.

I had to hear the finish of this story, for my own well-being.

"What was it that was so memorable?"

"At the reception, there was this elderly man, at least elderly to a five year old; he was probably eighty or so. This old man was very distinctive looking, kind of like that old guy in the American Gothic picture, or painting, or whatever the hell that is...just one of the reasons why I remember him. I was out in the lobby by the restrooms and my two brothers and I were messing around on this wrought iron railing that separated two staircases when we noticed this man with his salty white hair and his drawn pallor face. I remember he had obscenely long ears, and an even more obscenely colored suit...shit brown. He commanded our attention, but only got mine and not my brothers.' I looked at him and he said 'Hey sweetheart, you want to see a trick?' He was a perfectly benign fellow, I could sense that, and it was one of my relative's weddings, so I didn't harbor any foreboding thoughts. Innocently, yet eagerly, I nodded my head. Since my brothers recognized that the man was now only interested in showing me the trick, because they did not give him their attention when asked, the two returned to their cavorting on the stairs and railing; they were still keeping a tab on me, though, and watching him out of the corner of their eyes. 'Watch closely now' the old man instructed. I squinted my eyes and focused them tightly. The old man brought both of his hands together in front of him like this..." Ella illustrated the action as she continued, "And then, seemingly clasped his left forefinger around his right thumb...and Pop! Just like that, he removed half of his thumb completely off of the other half still attached to his hand and then miraculously reattached it. At first, I froze. I thought my eyes had deceived me. But when he repeated the trick several times in a row, I shrieked and ran off in search of my daddy..."

The whole table hunched over with laughter, especially Ella.

"It's not funny, really. The vision of that old man removing his thumb like that, with such ease, haunted me for weeks. It wasn't until my daddy explained to me exactly how the trick worked that I was finally able to get a good night's sleep." She concluded.

This sent the table reeling. We were uncontrollable.

"That old coot." Johnny added, which only made our insides ache even harder.

"Looks like these hussies are having fun, hey Clifton?" A recognizable voice cut through the laughter.

This was followed by, "Sure do, what do you say we show them the real meaning of fun, and take them away from these fairies."

I had turned around when I heard the first voice interrupt, but I noticed Ella had not. It was only when the second one joined in that she turned around...and in that moment, even the legitimate fight she witnessed earlier could not have prepared her for the destructive force that lay within Johnny's fists.

Instantly, he hurled them upon the first man, Charlie, knocking him hard to his back after a lethal combination to the face. I heard the women shrill with fright, probably for Charlie and Clifton...or maybe because they didn't believe a human being was capable of what they were witnessing Johnny do.

Clifton, the man who was behind the one currently on the floor, tried to retrieve a butterfly knife from his blue jeans, but was futile in his attempt. Johnny had broken his arm before the man's fingers could even brush the cold steel casing of the knife protruding from his back pocket. Clifton winced in sheer agony, but Johnny did not allow him to fall to the floor. Instead, he drove the man's head into the wall with such force that it indented the drywall severely; hair follicles remained lodged within chipped paint as he retracted the man's head. Blood started to flow from Clifton's eye and mouth as Ella finally realized the magnitude of Johnny's power. She began to plead for the two men.

By this time, Charlie, the man who was knocked to the floor, struggled to his feet by aid of one of the barstools. He picked the barstool up end over end and rushed Johnny with it.

Johnny let Clifton's body fall limp to the floor as he heard Charlie behind him and anticipated his rush. Johnny dropped to his feet as the chair was hurled over top of him. It hit the wall and grazed Clifton's head as it found the floor. Johnny knocked Charlie's feet out from under him with a swipe of his right leg and jumped on top of the man to finish the job.

Then, a piercing noise resonated through the bar, and The Hill seemed to be rendered motionless by its sound.

Jane was gripping a black, Forty-Four Magnum in her right hand. She had it pointed at the ceiling. Plaster-wall particles floated in the air above her. There was a faint contrail of smoke oozing out of the gun. "That's enough Johnny. I don't want you killing those boys…they're good paying customers." Then, she glanced over at an inflated man who was standing…or more like shivering…in shock at the far end of the bar. "Some bouncer you are Ferguson. Now get yourself together and remove those two men and don't let them back in tonight."

Ferguson hesitantly approached Johnny, who still pinned Charlie beneath him. Ferguson stopped when he noticed Ella coming over to take Johnny away.

Ella suggested that it was time for all of us to leave.

As the rest of us gathered ourselves, Johnny threw down a fifty-dollar bill on top of the table we were drinking at. "That's for the wall Jane, I'm sorry but you know there was nothing I could do."

"Can't deny a man his true nature, right Johnny?"

Johnny smiled as the four of us left The Hill.

Chapter 7

I had been to Jackie Blasé's apartment twice before, both on social occasions where many other people were present. I don't remember it being as dull and as featureless as it was now. The state of mind I was in didn't help matters, and it certainly affected my perspective. I felt empty.

I didn't regret waking up next to Jackie as much as I regretted not feeling bad about it. She was still asleep. The drinks last night had persuaded us all differently, but with the same potency. I had never thought about intimacy with Jackie until last night, after I met Ella. Something strange always seems to transpire when the human mind tries to rationalize, and make sense out of, the human heart and the emotions derived from it.

Jackie looked as delicate and as fragile as I had ever noticed her before, turned over to one side with her porcelain skin only half covered by the duvet. I brushed her auburn hair out of her face with a gentle stroke of my hand and forgot about all of her shortcomings that annoyed me so tenaciously…for the moment. She was beautiful.

A wall clock above the refrigerator told me it was a quarter until ten o'clock as I departed Jackie's apartment. My place was only a few blocks away, and I rather welcomed the genial sunshine as it accompanied me on my jaunt home. I decided to give Johnny a ring after I showered and readied myself for the day.

"Hey, do you want to go grab a bite to eat?" I asked. I heard Ella giggling in the background.

Johnny took a moment to answer. "Hold on my boy…let me see if Ella wants to join us."

Subconsciously, I wanted her to join us, because I wanted to get as much of her as I could in hopes of one day winning her, but consciously, I was infuriated by the notion. When Johnny returned he said, " It looks like it's just the two of us."

I imagined he could sense my contempt when I did not respond accordingly and aptly. "Meet me at Willie's in thirty…how's that sound?"

Johnny knew my car was still in the shop. Willie's was a diner right down the street from my apartment complex. They had the best chicken fried steak in the whole city.

"That's fine. I'll see you soon."

We hung up together and then I lit a cigarette. I grabbed my billfold and then exited my apartment. I headed towards Willie's. I knew I would arrive at the eatery well before Johnny since it was only a twelve minute walk from my place, but I needed some time alone with a cup of coffee and some cigarettes to gather my thoughts and possibly deflect any more of them (concerning Ella) from entering with merciless intensity. It would be an attempt at countervailing with caffeine and tobacco along with the down home, musty atmosphere of Willie's Diner. I desperately needed to regrind myself in fear of losing control of my emotions altogether. Dreading that just the mere sight of my best, and only, friend would send my thoughts a jumping, I knew I needed to prepare myself, and it would be futile (not to mention gross mismanagement of my thoughts and time) if we ended up arriving at the same moment.

The waiter was overweight and pockmarked. He was perfect...exactly what I needed.

"Coffee, sir?"

"Please." I grinned at him as I smashed my cigarette out in the black plastic ashtray. I quickly drew another one.

I noticed him notice my smile. He looked at me awkwardly and said, "Do I know you, sir?"

I shook my head silently, and with my wry grin still on my face and the cigarette smoke starting to become a nuisance for the waiter, I responded, "I come up here from time to time. I just live right down the street at The Crux apartments."

The waiter nodded his head slowly, still looking at me with one wary eye. "Cream or sugar?"

"No thanks, Ernie..." A brown nametag with white lettering embossed on it displayed his appellation. "I like it dark, just like the aura of this place."

"Whatever." Ernie said with minor disgust.

I laughed.

"Here's a menu."

"Thank you. We're going to need two...I'm waiting for a friend."

"I'm sure you are." Ernie slapped another menu down in front of the empty seat across from me, and then walked off. I noticed him shaking his head as he did so.

I laughed again.

Thoughts of society filled my conscious mind. And with great pleasure I pondered them repeatedly, applying my realistic ideologies to each one that exploded in my head. These thoughts had succeeded in pushing thoughts of Ella right back into the corner of my brain that was temporarily inaccessible. This process went on for ten full minutes, until it all came crashing down when I heard the bell jingle from the opening of the glass-entry door. It was Johnny. He looked to have more vigor than usual, considering what he went through last night; it was impressive to see him looking the way he did.

A few of the diner's patrons turned to look at him as his presence commanded attention. He sat down with a half scowl smeared on his face.

"Hey." I said.

"What was that all about?"

Nothing like starting your morning off with Johnny getting right down to it. Small talk was idle and pointless with him. Johnny had sensed my apprehension over the phone. I had expected this, and I had the ability to placate Johnny rather easily because he trusted me. "You mean the hesitation when it came to mention of Ella joining us?"

Johnny nodded his head feverishly. "Yeah, that's what I mean!"

"Calm down, Johnny. I think she's great...too great! I'm sorry about that. I guess I was still shaking off the cobwebs from last night. Johnny, Ella is a great woman, truly, and you're a very lucky man. You deserve her...now here, have a cigarette and hold any aggression inside for tonight."

Johnny smiled as I threw my pack of cigarettes in front of him. He took one and lit it. Then he said, "You stayed at Jackie's last night, didn't you?"

All my mind was thinking of was Ella, but I did manage to reveal a smile of guilt in response to Johnny's question.

"You old coot. I knew the two of you were going to get together...she worships the ground you walk on, you know? Don't ask me why, but she does."

I chuckled that last statement off. Momentarily, I didn't want to consider Jackie Blasé's misconceptions of grandeur, which somehow she felt I portrayed or had the capability of fulfilling. "Let's not talk about meaningless, lustful escapades obviously originating and consequently peregrinating from cheap vodka, to my blood, then to my brain, and then into Jackie's bedroom. It was completely beyond my control."

"Yeah right. I know exactly where those meaningless, lustful emotions originated from and traveled to." Johnny replied.

We laughed together.

The waiter showed up and began to pour Johnny a cup of coffee. Strangely, and impolitely, I noticed both of us were still occupied by laughter. "Johnny, meet Ernie."

I couldn't resist (anything to keep my mind off Ella). This propelled my laughter to a higher level. Ernie looked down at me with disdain. Johnny played along. He extended his hand and Ernie took it in confused anger. "I'll tell you what Ernie, instead of coffee, how about getting me a shot of Goldshlager?" Ernie furrowed his eyebrows with even more confusion, as Johnny added, "Nothing like getting the day started with an element!"

I couldn't control myself, and I was consciously aware that although we were jovially messing around with Ernie, our waiter, I couldn't help but notice our misguided unintentional remarks had the opposite effect on him. Ernie looked down at the ground in embarrassment.

Ironically, this made me think of Ella, and how she would ruefully look down upon our conduct. I felt even emptier now, as I halted my laughter.

I looked up at Ernie and prepared to express my condolences, but Johnny beat me to it. He grabbed Ernie by the arm. "Hey Ernie, listen man, Emerson over there doesn't mean anything by it, and I certainly don't either. We are sincerely sorry. We both had a rough night last night. Will you accept our apology?" Ernie looked over at me with hesitation and then nodded his head. "Thank you." Johnny concluded.

I averted my eyes. I was the one feeling humiliated, now. I felt like running straight out of Willie's and into the arms of Jackie, whose blind, unrestrained craving for my acceptance, approval, and acquaintance would suitably squelch my feelings of inadequacy towards my fellow man, but the situation rendered my presence, and my vain hopes were routed by Ella's scold as displayed through Johnny's eyes, all the while giving him a free pass.

"Coffee is fine man. And actually, while you're here, we might as well go ahead and place our order…" Johnny looked over at me for confirmation of readiness. I nodded my head. "I'll take three eggs over-easy…three slices of bacon, crispy…and three pieces of brown toast, burnt."

Ernie jotted Johnny's order down on his little notepad, and then focused on me. "I'll take the chicken fried steak…please." I feared my food would be purposefully contaminated, with stuff I'd rather not think about, but it was too late now.

"Anything else?"

"No. That's fine Ernie. Thank you." Johnny was being exceptionally polite, for he knew that his earlier crack had contradicted one of his principles; he had treated Ernie unjustly, and he regretted it, so he made up for it by consideration for Ernie in hopes of winning his confidence back…and he had. I was not so lucky, and it was evident Ernie did not hold me in the same regard as Johnny.

Even when he was the purveyor of injustice, Johnny was capable of righting it swiftly upon himself, just as he would another, in order to keep his integrity.

"So number two is tonight?" I said, desiring to forget about the situation collectively.

"Yeah. I've got this Mexican fellow named 'Hector The

Snake.' I don't know his last name, or if he even has one. We go on second. Fights start at eight o'clock again tonight. I can't wait…The Snake will be a worm after I get done with him. You're coming, right?"

"Wouldn't miss it, Johnny."

I smiled and hoped I didn't reveal my soul.

"Good." He finished.

My heart raced, as I knew in just under ten hours I would be entering extremely dangerous, uncharted waters.

The rest of the morning, including my meal, was a conscious blur. My awareness was limited to one thing the rest of the day, and leading into the evening: the knowledge of aloneness with Ella.

Chapter 8

Her car reminded me of a movie I had seen as I child with my father. The movie was about a loner who raced cars in order to gain acceptance from his peers. The car the loner drove was silver and black, just as Ella's was. The interior leather of Ella's car was cracked and worn, which gave it a sense of wisdom, as if the car itself was too smart to let another one crash into it. It was the safest car I had ever been in.

"I like the feel of this car…security. I like that." I said as we pulled away from the front of The Crux apartment complex.

Ella looked over and drew a smile for me. Immediately, I writhed in the seat with uneasiness. I searched for a cigarette to calm myself down. "I like you Emerson. You're unlike any man I have ever known."

I rubbed the top of my forehead in disarray. I couldn't decipher her sincerity, if any. I felt helpless in the presence of this woman, and it was incredibly liberating.

"You're like no other woman I have ever known…that's for sure." I replied. I thought of that old proverb: When in Rome…

"So tell me Ella, what did you think of last night?"

She looked at me out of the corner of her eye; I was unable

to discern if suspicion or curiosity lurked beneath it.

"I don't think I have ever seen such a display of raw energy and pure power." She answered.

"I was referring to The Hill."

"Me too."

We shared a laugh.

"You know Emerson, I have never seen that side of Johnny before, probably because over the summer it was just him and I hanging out together, with no one else to interfere, so we weren't really exposed to a situation like last night. But I'll tell you, I found it horrifying, yet extremely arousing…in a Marquis de Sade sort of way."

"I didn't figure you for sadism."

"Maybe I phrased that improperly. Johnny's unrefined power is undeniable in its sexuality, and that is what turns me on."

"I didn't figure you for feminism, either."

"There's a difference between existentialism and feminism. A vast difference."

I smiled at her. "So you believe in the freedom of your choice and responsibility for the consequences, if any, of that choice."

"Precisely."

"What if the choice is made for you?"

"What do you mean?"

"For example, what if I leaned over and kissed you…"

She looked at me warily, but kept one eye on the road. "Then you would find out what my choice would be in response to that. I could choose to kick you out of my car and tell Johnny, or I could choose to go along with it. No matter which one, the emphasis of my response will still be directly related to the uniqueness and isolation of the experience…right here and now. And, the guilt in which I would or would not be free from is relative to that choice."

I stared into her eyes as she looked over at me. Volatility filled the air between us. My palms began to sweat. The cars outside on the highway raced by us like we were the pace car and the caution flag had just been lifted. The empty feeling I had succumbed to all day was washed out by vitality and reality.

"But you're not going to do that now, are you? You are too scared of the consequences, and the responsibility that goes along with them. You're a realist Emerson."

The empty feeling returned so rapidly that I literally felt the air being sucked out of my lungs.

"That's why I like you. You're predictable, safe, unwavering in conscience…that's why I like you." Ella finished.

She notice my eyes glaze over with the truth of twenty-one years of lost experience hidden beyond. Fear had ruled my life, and Ella had just made that permanent denial an unwanted acceptance. The epiphany was bitter and I was glad we were almost at the Red Rocks.

Because of her compassionate heart, Ella felt the need to apologize. But it was unneeded and unnecessary. She was an incredibly great woman.

Chapter 9

The massive boulders that engulfed the concrete bleachers gave me a feeling of darkness that I likened to the Middle Ages. I had returned to my empty state, but it was welcomed. In fact, it was significant in the way it allowed me to understand. Ella had inspired me to gain a new perspective...a different perspective. One of which I had previously been unable to tap into because I was unaware of the enormity of its existence. Of course, this realization was just that, nothing more.

The crowd was substantially larger today than yesterday, and based on some of the ramblings I had been overhearing for the past half hour word has gotten around about Johnny. This was not surprising...but the way it made me feel was. I wasn't as proud for him today as I was yesterday, or any other day before that. I wasn't as proud to boast him my friend. Disconnection entered as my mind became indubitably complicated. I shook my head furiously to straighten out the string of thoughts that had jumbled up, coiled on top of and around one another, and caused me to feel the way I felt. Overabundance was about. But, overabundance of what?

"What's up Emerson...are you okay?" Ella asked with

genuine concern. We were sitting side by side, and she placed her left arm around me.

"Sure. Just a little bit of a pain up top…trying to shake it loose."

"That's too bad. Is there anything I can do…I believe I've got some aspirin in my purse."

"No, that's alright Ella. It's not that type of ache. Aspirin won't help."

"Oh." She zipped her purse back up and replaced her arm around me. She had a comforting touch.

The pain was starting to fade away, at least for the time being.

"You're a lot like me Emerson. I get those types of pains every once in a while too. You know what I do about it to help forget?"

"What's that?"

"I take a shot of whiskey…" We both chuckled. "Then I take another."

"Unfortunately, we don't have any whiskey." I said as I looked over at her.

"That's true, but how about a beer?"

I smiled at her as the pain left me for good.

"Great. I'll go get us a couple." Ella patted me on the back twice, consolingly, and then meandered up to the landing to get us a couple of beers.

I mused of a life together with her. I pictured the two of us slowly swinging back and forth on our white hammock nestled between two sturdy oaks, conversing about life's leading and most thought-provoking questions: 'What do you think the kids are up to right now?' 'What do you think of the current administration…truthfully?' 'Do you think I look good with these sunglasses on, or better with them off?' Each answer being topped off with a subtle, sincere kiss. It was cruel in its natural simplicity and primitiveness, and that's what made it fantastic and beautiful and perfect. There was no doubt whatsoever, anymore, that I was in love with this woman. I believe the Italians have a saying for it, something along the lines of getting struck by lightning…well I have, two days in a row, and those bolts continue to be thrust upon me.

I fear, each and everyday that passes by in the same fashion as today has passed, a mutual friendship because of our affection for another: Johnny. Only, her affinity for Johnny is obviously very different than mine. I was beginning to hurt again.

"Here you go. I got you two. Drink the first one down really fast. I promise it will get rid of your aching head."

At that moment, I realized, and understood, it was not my head that was aching. "Thank you Ella. You're a kind, wonderful woman."

"I know."

We shared a laugh and then a drink. Then I did as she instructed and slammed the rest of my first beer down.

"Hey look, there's my boy." Ella pointed Johnny out. Interesting that she chose those words to refer to him. He was talking with Percy Leonne.

I'm sure there wasn't much instruction from Percy, for he now understood clearly that all Johnny needed to do was be himself, and he would come out the victor…something Percy realized last night.

The fight that was currently underway was in its fifth round, and it seemed the boxer in the red corner, Jackson, was about to prevail. The blue corner fighter was weak in the knees and his swollen eyes were too much of a hindrance to get past in order to put up either a good defense or a good offense. I reckoned it would be over in the next round.

"What do you want to do with your life Emerson?" Ella's

question made me pause in mid-drink. It took me completely off guard.

"I don't know."

"Come on, you've at least given it some thought, right?"

"Yeah, I guess I've thought a little about it." The line of questioning had made me very uncomfortable.

"What do you want to do?" I asked Ella. I was hoping to redirect the questions that inspired my discomfort.

"I'm going to be a Drifter…a professional Drifter." She laughed.

I returned the favor. "Seriously?"

"Seriously." She stated.

"And what is it that is required of one in order to achieve this professional status?"

"A heart Emerson. A strong, blood-pumping heart. That's it." Her poignancy was skillfully masked by grace.

We shared another drink as I mulled the subtleties over. "What does the job entail?"

"Great, soulful rewards. Rewards you can't find in any other profession…just about."

"You mind sharing with me some of these rewards?"

"It's the code of the Drifter's ethics not to share with those who doubt."

"I don't doubt."

"Sure you do, or else you would be a professional Drifter."

"Then that means you must doubt too, or else you would already be one."

"Unfortunately, you're right. I still have a little doubt, but I feel that with the right Drifting mate, or partner, than that would be all I need to cast the insecurities I hold towards the profession off."

"Like a man?"

"Sure."

"Like Johnny?"

"I don't know. Maybe...maybe not."

I considered the possibilities, as I once again found myself in a comparable situation to the one on the car ride up. The implications were exceedingly extensive, however, with this current predicament. I needed to choose my words proficiently and effectively.

Ella continued, "Why do you think I'm in Denver in the first place? It's not to go to art school...I'll tell you that. It's to find my soulmate, Emerson. The one who will Drift with me throughout this journey we call Life."

"I thought you enjoyed your art, and the art school? At least that's what it sounded like last night."

"I do, thoroughly. But I would consider art a companion, not a component of life's journey. One's mate, or partner, along with one's own harmonious heart are the only components one really needs...uh-oh, I just slipped. I broke the basic code of the Drifter's ethics. You've got to promise me, you will not tell anybody, who is not capable of understanding of course, about what I just told you."

Her ability to manipulate my mind was staggering, so much so that I stood up to take another drink and steady myself. "I promise...but what if one can become in tune with one's soul without the aid or help of a mate, or partner, or component, in the form of a literal companion?"

"If one is happy being alone, then there is no problem. But, no doubt, one will only realize it if it is a mistake...after it's too late. Once you've made the choice to be a Drifter, and fully commit yourself to it, then you can't ever go back."

I believe I understood what she was spewing. We touched beer cups as I offered gratitude for her explanation.

"But, back to you Emerson, you did not answer me the question: What do you want to do when you get out of here?"

Proficiently and effectively, I answered, "Drift."

Chapter 10

'Hector The Snake' lasted only twenty four seconds longer than Freddie 'Fingers.' After what happened to 'Fingers,' 'Hector The Snake' thought it would be to his advantage to try and dance his way to victory. Johnny's footwork was just as impressive as his might, though, and The Snake soon found himself backed into a corner enduring three left jabs and one final devastating blow in the form of a right uppercut. Not soon after this bout, Percy Leonne found 'The Aussie' moving in on his territory. Johnny laughed this off and let the trainer and the promoter go at it...verbally. By the time we left the event, 'The Aussie' and Percy were sitting next to one another discussing possible future routes to be ventured with their new find. Both of them, but more notably 'The Aussie,' took time to see all three of us off. They were smiling uncontrollably.

"Has Emerson moved in on you yet?" Johnny joked as we headed out of the foothills and back to town. Our destination this night was Zany Blue, a dark lounge that specialized in smoky jazz. I was rather looking forward to relaxing there, especially after the stimulating scene last night at The Hill. Johnny and Ella were looking forward to it as well.

I shrugged in the backseat and let out a sigh of disbelief and disgust. I had never done anything in the past to prompt Johnny to quip such a remark. And of the few qualities that became of Johnny, witty banter was not one of them. It suddenly occurred to me that my reactions, or non-reactions, in the present were what instigated this glib.

"Oh yeah, you're done for, it's me and Emerson from here on out. I'm dropping you off at the first street corner."

Johnny looked back at me, and then over at his girl. He smiled as he thought of a response. I smiled too, for I appreciated the genuineness of Ella's ease of offhand conversation over the fabrication of Johnny's. The only thing Johnny could think of to reply with was throwing his right hand playfully over the seat directed towards my jaw. My artificial smiled showed my true emotions, and Johnny didn't leave it unnoticed. He looked at me tightly before he turned around to face Ella again. Ella had not picked up on it, but she could feel the tension that had just flooded the confined space of the sports car we were traveling in.

The lounge was ten minutes away, and nervousness crept closer at the thought…until Ella's maneuverable interjection. "Johnny, tell me that story you alluded to last night but never got around to telling…the one about when you and Emerson first met."

Johnny looked back at me, and the both of us painfully restrained our facial muscles to keep from smiling. I noticed Ella smiling through the rearview mirror at me. The numerous constructive traits she possessed were so honest it was hard to choose which one was the most endearing.

"Emerson had arrived a day before me. I came to the university by way of charter bus. I had the driver drop me off in the back parking lot behind my designated dorm, which happened to be the same building as Emerson's. He must have been bored or alone or something, because I noticed him looking out his dorm window at me as I departed the bus. I was a hostile person back then..." Ella and I laughed at Johnny's mockery.

I felt inclined in keeping with the story, so I said, "Back then!"

"I still am a hostile person...but I have learned to manifest it properly."

Ella and I laughed again; mine was a little harder than hers. Johnny was trying to fool himself, more so than either one of us. He joined us as he failed. "Anyways, I didn't like the way Emerson was looking at me, so I dropped my bag right there in the parking lot and yelled up to him 'Why don't you come down off that damn perch of yours and stare at me like that face to face...you damn Bird!'"

Ella turned quickly to Johnny. My boisterous laughter bellowed in the background as Johnny struggled to keep a straight face. "You damn Bird!" Ella wanted to make sure her ears had not deceived her.

"That's right, the S.O.B. called me a Bird." I threw in for good measure.

Ella busted out.

"What? It was a long bus ride...this skinny little dark haired Romeo looking guy was hanging out his window like I was Juliet or something, and the way his body was positioned and contorted on the sill reminded me of a lark perched atop a Birch tree..."

I didn't have the heart to tell Johnny he had the Shakespearean character's roles mixed; plus it was rather humorous. "Contorted? I was straddling the sill smoking a cigarette. I was respecting my roommate's request not to smoke...at least partially."

"I don't remember seeing a cigarette."

"That's because when you uttered the most asinine and uncalled for remark I had ever heard, it took me so far aback, I dropped the cigarette down to ground."

"Whatever!"

"In addition, to set the record straight, I was admiring the bus, not you my friend."

Johnny turned around matter-of-factly and said, "It was a nice bus wasn't it?" We nodded to one another in deferential agreement, and then he continued, "Anyways, Romeo here..."

Ella looked hard at Johnny. She needed some expounding on Johnny's biting label of me. "Romeo? Why Romeo?"

"Cause he's a good looking guy...come on Emerson, don't play coy."

I remained silent, as I waited Ella's response. I caught her smile out of the corner of her mouth through the rearview mirror; it was the corner opposite Johnny. Ella and I locked eyes through the mirror.

"Come on just admit it Emerson, you're a good looking guy...it's nothing to be ashamed of." Johnny was trying to purposefully embarrass me, for he sensed a slight connection between Ella and I. He knew I knew I was handsome, and he also knew I was embarrassed about it. I felt blood rushing to my face as his seemingly inadvertent ploy (for Ella) worked. Ella averted her eyes from the mirror and back onto the road as she felt my self-consciousness.

Damn Johnny! He always knew how to get the upper hand. Even when he was wrong he always seemed to make himself look right.

"You know that old Romeo and Juliet movie done by that famous Italian director...the one they show you in elementary school?" Johnny added.

Ella nodded her head with affirmation, and Johnny continued, "Doesn't Emerson look like Romeo...void of the olive skin?"

I planned to keep my eyes lowered, but irrepressibly, and instinctively, they locked with Ella's in the mirror again. Johnny looked over at Ella, momentarily. She seemed to be oblivious to him.

He recognized his mistake as he quickly resumed the story. "Anyways, so Emerson, my boy..." Johnny turned to me with thrashing eyes, intending to remind me that he was in control and that Ella was his girl. He didn't achieve his desired effect. "...yells back down to me, 'Did you just call me a Bird? I have been called names before in the past, but I have never been referred to as a Bird...that's got to be the nicest insult I have ever heard, if indeed that is what it was.' I had to contain my pending smile. My affront had been reduced and twisted into a compliment. Then he told me to 'Hold on.' He disappeared from the window, and two minutes later arrived at the back entrance to the dorm. He held the door open for me and stated, 'Well, come on, I'll help you in.' I didn't much feel like hurting him after that...in fact, I befriended him."

"Since then, we've been great friends." I added.

Johnny leaned back and saw an opportunity. He took it and offered me his hand. "The greatest."

I shook it and immediately retreated my thoughts back to a hidden spot within my conscience, hoping never to let them back out.

"That's a nice story...a really nice story. I'm better off for knowing it. What other stories do you two have?"

"Trust me, you don't want to know the half of them." Johnny said as he turned back around and faced forward.

"That's for sure." I added.

Silence fell over the car as everybody brought themselves back down to reality.

We arrived at the lounge without another word spoken.

A wrinkly, grizzled drum man was fanning the cymbals with his brush stick as a coarse-voiced, sleek-skinned vocalist murmured veritable jazz lyrics with a bluesy undertone. The place occupied fifty-to-sixty at maximum capacity, and we were pleasantly surprised to find that it was only half full on this Saturday evening. I ordered the drinks while Johnny and Ella chose an isolated section behind, and to the left, of the duet. I noticed a trombone setting off to the side of the stage, leaning against a support. The duet was actually a trio, and the horn player was on the other end of the bar picking up on two voluptuous, mahogany-skinned ladies. I reveled in his 'coolness' for a moment before I turned and walked back to Johnny and Ella with the drinks.

A half-moon, purple velvet divan, with a pearl white, all-ceramic cylinder table resting in the middle of it, was the ensemble of furniture in the section Johnny and Ella chose to sit at. I handed the drinks off to them accordingly and lit a cigarette before I sat down.

I noticed the vocalist staring at me. She was very striking. I smiled at her and she returned the gesture.

"You see Ella...Romeo I tell you!"

"I thought we already went over this. Not again, please." I said as I adjusted myself between the fluffy pillows on the backless couch.

"You're right my boy...how about this one, then?"

I looked over at Johnny with consumed interest. He made sure Ella was listening closely. Johnny leaned forward and so did I. "As both of you know, I'm going to win that boxing contest tomorrow."

"That was a given when you entered Johnny, I knew that."

"Exactly Emerson, but what you didn't know was what I planned on doing with my half of the prize money..."

"That's true." I looked across at Ella. She remained silent

with aroused curiosity.

Johnny took a drink from his highball and then recoiled back to the comfort of velvet and feathery pillows. I remained leaning forward, and now Ella had assumed the same position on her side of the divan.

"What are you going to do with it Johnny?" She begged.

Johnny smirked, and then said, "When I was young, and before I knew better, my father took me on one of his business trips to New York..."

I looked across at Ella and she looked back at me...just the mention of New York got our blood flowing. I had never been there, and I could tell by Ella's reaction that neither had she. I could also tell that she held the city in the same esteem that I did. Our giddiness translated into inescapable grins. This affected Johnny, and he thoroughly delighted in the moment.

"The first, and best memory was of the ironic perspective of speed. The way the natives tactically jockeyed themselves amongst one another throughout the bustle of the city with such grace and ease and beauty made everything seem as if it was surreal. It overwhelmed me, for the city seemed inaccessible, almost beyond reach, and I appeared to be just a blink in its massive eye. I remember feeling so small in a place so big..." Johnny paused to reflect. "It was great. Unfortunately, I also remember what happened the three ensuing days with my trusty companion..." Johnny's facetiousness was unsuccessful at hiding his anguish.

Ella did not understand, and she looked over at me for help. I caught her out of the corner of my eye, but I remained focused on Johnny. I had never been privileged the details of the trip he was referring to, nor do I believe it would be a privilege, but I knew of his old man and I knew of the way he treated Johnny as a youngster, and that was all I needed to know. I felt sympathy for Ella and her confusion, but if Johnny had not revealed his relationship with his father to her, then that was his prerogative, and I certainly was not going to meddle.

"But I will spare you the details out of respect for your, and my, humanity and decency. The point is that I want to experience the great city, as an adult now, the way it was intended to be experienced..." Johnny paused and reflected again.

"Next weekend, I'm taking all of us to New York!" He finished.

Ella wrapped her arms tightly around Johnny. She couldn't contain her delight, nor did she want to.

"I've already made all the arrangements. We are going to leave Friday morning and come back Sunday morning. Were staying two nights in the city that never sleeps!" Johnny could not contain his elation either. He picked Ella up and swung her around while she kissed him and held him close.

I focused on the vocalist, for I wanted someone to share the excitement with. She looked at me provocatively and licked her lips sensually.

"Oh yeah, and Emerson, my boy, I got four tickets. You can take Jackie...or whoever."

I turned around to make sure I heard him correctly. It would be a cold day below before I took Jackie Blasé to New York. I returned my attention to the jazz singer. After her set concluded, I walked up to her with a scotch and soda. "Do you want to go to New York?"

Chapter 11

The final bout was scheduled for seven o'clock Sunday evening. 'The Aussie' had a small entourage consisting of two news reporters and two fellow promoters. He eagerly awaited promotion of the winner, which of course would be Johnny. 'The Aussie' would promote the fighter Down Under first and get Johnny some valued experience before he brought him back over to the States. But 'The Aussie' was not imprudent or unwise, he knew where the money was, and if the price was right he would be more than willing to keep Johnny right here in the States and 'set him out for slaughter' against a real heavyweight contender…at least so he thought; slaughter wasn't something Johnny incurred, it was something he inflicted. Even with his fine display in this contest, Johnny still would not be considered a legitimate contender until he started getting some 'real' fights under his belt. This contest was even below an exhibition, so it was understandable why 'The Aussie' thought the way he thought, just like everyone else. I had no doubts though, and neither did Johnny, which was all that was important.

It was a little cooler this night than the previous two, and the penetration of the brisk air into my lungs was inviting. I instructed Ella to stand up from the bleacher and join me in a cigarette. "Isn't it a lovely night, Ella?"

"Most definitely. Not a cloud in the sky, stars shining bright, and my Johnny boy is getting ready to beat old Jackson right out of these mountains."

I enjoyed her enthusiasm.

I pulled the smoke into my lungs and savored the taste as long as my oxygen supply would allow, for the contradiction of tobacco with the refreshing mountain air was immensely pleasurable.

"How long do you think Jackson is going to last?" I asked.

"Two rounds."

"You think? I bet he'll take him out in the first, just like 'Fingers' and The Snake."

"Maybe so, but either way it's not going to last long, which is good because I'm a little cool." Ella had her hands wrapped around her upper arms. She was wearing a denim shirt with denim jeans and cowboy boots, but she had forgot her coat in the car. I offered her mine. She smiled and said, "No that's okay Emerson, you need your jacket...plus, the frigidness just gives me an excuse to pull this out..."

Ella opened her purse up and pulled out a fifth of Jack Daniels. She took a snort and then handed the bottle off to me. Ironically, the chilled air intensified the harshness of the whiskey as it slid down my throat. I winced it down to my stomach and then handed the bottle back to her.

"Feels good, doesn't it?" Ella asked rhetorically as she took another pull.

"Look, the fight's getting ready to commence." I directed Ella's attention towards the ring. She was already focused on it.

"Let's remain standing...it's nice to stand. Anyways, there's nobody behind us." She suggested.

I looked at her and wondered if there was an ulterior motive other than comfort. She smiled at me without blatancy as she kept her eyes on the ring and the man inside of it.

Jackson looked to be twice Johnny's weight, and if it weren't for the pamphlet we received on Friday night giving us the accurate dimensions of each fighter, I would have for sure assumed Jackson was well over three hundred and fifty pounds. He appeared as big as the mountains that surrounded us. At first, I felt moderately concerned for Johnny, which was notable, because I had never had that feeling for him before, but as I watched Jackson dance around the ring throwing mock combinations in Johnny's direction as he was introduced, my nerves were immediately settled, because one of Johnny's previous opponents had made the same mistake two nights before…surely Jackson couldn't have forgotten what happened to him?

"Isn't it divine of Johnny to take us to New York next weekend?" Ella asked as she took another pull off her whiskey bottle.

"He's a true friend."

I recognized her looking over at me with interest. I looked back over at her. There was a moment of enigmatic silence that laid way to anxiousness. I grabbed the bottle of whiskey out of her hand and took another hit; this one was easier to throw down.

"Indeed, the truest of friends." She stated plainly as she remained focused on me.

"You're an interesting soul Emerson Parks, very interesting. I believe I might just make a Drifter out of you yet." She added as she leaned in closer to me.

The bell to initiate the boxing match rang. Neither one of us swayed in our focus upon one another. I leaned in closer to her as thoughts of betrayal bombarded the front of my head, while thoughts of love bombarded the back of my heart.

Was losing Johnny a proviso to winning this girl? Of course it was!

I thought of our conversation yesterday about existentialism, and I thought of Ella's theory on the Drifter's code of ethics. My palms had never before accumulated so much moisture. They were drenched. I could feel my fingertips and my toes tingling with sensation.

"I can see those wheels turning in there Emerson Parks…are they spinning thoughts of good or bad?"

Her breath tickled my nose as she spoke; whiskey and tobacco was an exotically alluring combination. If I just leaned forward a few more inches I could get a taste of heaven.

"Bad…very bad."

"Are you prepared to accept the consequences for your choices…your free choices?"

I closed my eyes and envisioned Johnny getting knocked out because he was frozen with shock at what his best friend…his greatest friend…was about to do to his girl.

When I reopened them I wrapped my arms tightly around her and said, "No." I could feel her smiling behind me. Underneath my breath, I murmured, "Not yet."

When we separated there was a mutual understanding between us: that neither one would speak of this instance again, unless revisited in the future (in which case it wouldn't be necessary to speak of it).

To my surprise, Jackson was still standing after the opening round's bell rung. His nose was oozing blood and appeared to be broken, but to his credit he was still standing. I took another hit of whiskey and then handed the bottle back to Ella.

"Wine is victimizing in its capacity to reveal heartfelt honesty." She spoke with a laugh. "Unfortunately, this is whiskey."

Her ability to confound my emotions with my logic was stunning in the aggravation I derived from it.

"So, are you going to take Jackie Blasé?" She asked with a hint of sarcasm as she sat back down on the bleacher.

I looked down at her disdainfully. "My hypocrisy only stretches so far…I'm constantly confined by limitations. I'm going to take Nena McCray."

"Who's that?"

"Remember the vocalist last night at the lounge?"

Ella's mouth dropped agape. "No way."

"Most definitely a goddess of the night she is…a goddess of the night. The perfect Drifting companion for New York…a true throwback." I pointedly tried to manipulate Ella's own emotions.

After a minute's hesitation, Ella responded, "Great…this trip is going to be marvelous. I'm happy Miss Nena made the cut over Jackie Blasé. Jackie's all wrong for you, you know?"

"I know." I felt Ella's eyes running up and over my face, but I did not give in. "You're going to miss Johnny knock him out." This comment snapped her interest away from me and back onto the bout.

As she turned, Johnny applied a body blow directly into Jackson's chest that made him stammer backwards into the ropes. Johnny finished him off with a straight right to the nose, ensuring that Jackson's nose was broken for good, if in fact it had not been before. The rest of the crowd soon followed our animated cheers; everyone pulled for Johnny because they knew he was something special and they understood the privilege to pugilism they had just witnessed. Ella and I both knew Johnny was something far more exceptional than that which could be restricted to a boxing ring.

The referee displayed Johnny's arm up high in the air, as the ring announcer proclaimed him the victor of the tournament. 'The Aussie' and Percy Leonne joined him in the ring. They both gloated over him obscenely as the ring announcer presented the trophy to Johnny along with his half of the earnings, in cash.

    The world was in desperate need of conquering.

Part Two
Chapter 12

Nena McCray had spent time in New York once before, about ten years ago when she was first getting a hold on her jazz career. She was thirty back then. She claims to be much more cultivated now, but I still sense flashes of mad tendencies behind those big brown eyes. The only thing she spoke of remembering about her first trip was a neighborhood bar in Soho...one in which she had no qualms about frequenting. It was called Rollos back then, but she feared the place had changed names and possibly ownership when the cabbie looked at her incongruously.

The hotel we were keeping at was in The Village. It was reasonably inexpensive, and it showed. The only thing of extravagance, which it struggled to boast, was dated Spanish tile running down its narrow hallways. Our accommodations were not important however, Johnny had reiterated numerously, for we would only be sleeping there. He was right. Nine hundred dollars could only be stretched so far in New York. Nena and I were fortunate enough to have a room separate from Johnny and Ella.

We barely had a chance to settle in before Nena and Ella

suggested getting a drink. The two women had sat next to one another on the plane. It never seems to amaze me what the female persuasion is capable of when thrown together in tight quarters. They must have talked about everything under the sun during the abysmally long plane ride. And when we landed, they gave the impression of long lost friends. They really did have a lot in common, though, even if Nena was almost twice her age.

I considered Nena my ornament, and no doubt she considered me in the same method. We shared a mutual admiration in that way; we both perceived the other to embody what it was that we wanted out of a partner. I did not distinguish her sexually, however, although we had shared intimacy three times in the week before the trip. I was too weak to deny her the desires that yearned inside of her. Plus, it was shallowly fulfilling to be able to give a lonely soul pleasure, even if it was by means of physicality. We all needed something to hold onto.

Nena had been pushed around her whole life while growing up in the South and Midwest, until she found sanctity and salvation in Jazz. She studied the great voice of Eleanora 'Billie' Holiday and the composition style of William 'Count' Basie, and molded her own unique approach from their influences. She caught her first big break in Kansas City, on Vine Street, when she was twenty-five and hasn't been caught turning around ever since. She was not smart in the book sense, but it was obvious that she had compensated for her lack of education by way of the street. She was more sensible than Johnny, Ella, and myself combined. I found this grotesquely appealing as well as grotesquely threatening. I was proud to have her accompanying me, and Johnny and Ella were glad to have her along too.

Her chocolate colored hair ran down to the small of her

back, while her long, thick, bronze-colored legs made great effort to meet it; if it weren't for her curvy backside, this day covered by nothing but a black leather miniskirt, they would have succeeded. She wore an all-white blouse for a top, which emitted a touch of elegance to attempt to recompense her robust sex appeal. An intentional clash was waged when Nena chose to wear the clothes she wore, and the sultry side won out every time. That was the side I preferred (not in a sexual manner, but ironically, in an emotional manner).

The cabbie was a foreigner so it was conceivable he didn't even know how to navigate his yellow Oldsmobile to the Statue of Liberty without first having to consult with his map of New York City clipped to his sun visor. It was also quite possible that he didn't know any English, in which case it would be best if he just dropped us off in Times Square. But, Nena had a way about her. Semantics were not part of her upbringing, and language barriers did not exist with her. She was competent at communicating in many more ways than standard...and most definitively the verbal way wasn't even her most effective way. Nena had strategically chosen the front seat of the cab, while the rest of us had squeezed into the back. All four of us were already feeling pretty wound up from the libations we ordered to help pass the time on the flight, but Nena was feeling it the best. When the cabbie looked at her blankly at first mention of Rollos, Nena realized it was time to explain it in a different way. She lifted her skirt a few inches up her Amazonian legs. Instantly, the cabbie smiled. Nena smiled back, and then in a dash pulled the black skirt tightly against her legs.

"You know exactly what I'm talking about when it comes to that, don't you Shorty? You speak that language loud and clear! Now take us to Soho, the district with all the art and artists, and quit yankin' my chain!"

The cabbie obviously realized we were tourists, and Nena picked up on that. He didn't know what hit him. It turned out he spoke perfect English. Nena looked back at the three of us and cackled a laugh of satisfaction.

"No degrees needed here my college friends, Uh-Uh. Nothing but livin' boys…ain't that right Miss Ella?"

"Oh yeah."

The two women shared a friendly handshake as if they had just won a small battle in the war of the sexes. Johnny and I turned to one another and laughed out loud. Then, the ladies joined us. The cabbie remained silent, eyes straightforward.

"This is exactly what I'm talking about my friends…experience. We've only been in town an hour, and already it has been the best trip I have ever taken. Nena, I'm utterly grateful you are joining us. Might just be the best two hundred dollars I've ever spent." Johnny finished.

Nena smiled at him as Ella and I continued laughing in the background. This statement caused the cabbie to eye Johnny through the rearview mirror, and then focus on Nena again. The cabbie wasn't a cabbie for nothing.

Nena picked up on it and said, "Come on Shorty, you know better. These goods are not for sale! Don't think you're part of the conversation when you're not. Now, just put your eyes back on the road and don't try and take us for a ride, because I'll know if you do."

It was not surprising Nena was even stronger than Ella, for she had been on this earth many more years, but even Ella had to acknowledge her self-confidence and respect it gracefully. And, Ella was the type of woman that would gladly do so too. She wasn't like Jackie Blasé.

With the exception of the obvious physical difference, I imagined Ella to turn out to be exactly like Nena was, only with more scholarly refinement, when she reached her

Drift

age…and that made me covet her even more. I foresaw problems in the near future, and I was beginning to think it was a bad idea to have brought Nena. In fact, it might have been a bad idea for myself to come.

When we exited the cab, the authenticity of the town hit us like a freightliner. I imagined Johnny could not have felt this way when he came here as a child; it was impossible to absorb it all as an adult, much less a little boy. Fiction was nowhere to be found in this city, indeed it was nowhere to even be imagined. Anything and everything was abound.

At that moment, I realized the rest of America, and probably the rest of the world, took a back seat to this place. New York wasn't the escape from reality…New York wasn't the movie…New York wasn't the fantastic story of innocence and guilt and love and sorrow…the rest of the world was, and the thought of never going back flashed through my mind. It would be impossible for one to feel empty in a place like this.

Then, the moment passed.

Nena led us through bohemians and gypsies and lawyers and brokers. And it was only the middle of the afternoon. Nena was the only one who spoke as she led the rest of her blissfully awestruck companions through the district, but none of us were capable of listening to her because of our preoccupied hearts. We were all too amazed and mesmerized and excited by what we saw. Awesomeness was an understatement.

I wondered if Johnny felt invincible in a town like this. Of course he did, he had Ella by his side, and even New York could not transcend her. I reflected that she was one of the only women on the face of this earth that had that ability. I really loved her.

Nena seemed to know where she was going, or at least think she knew, but if she didn't we weren't going to care. This is exactly what Johnny came for, and this is why he brought his best friends along. Before we tried to find Rollos, if it even still existed, we decided to meander into a few galleries and check out some local art.

The first gallery we strolled into was right off the street corner. The art was way too contemporary, even for Ella to appreciate, and the four of us turned around after only two minutes of confused time spent. The second one was less offensive, or perhaps more easily deciphered, but it still had a major contemporary beat to it. There was a sculpture, to give it undue credit, of a stuffed camel with mannequin's legs in place of its real legs that greeted each person as they entered. There were some writings on the wall in red, to the left, intending to look like blood but not being too effectual at it. And to the right, hung the most interesting display. There were five black and white photographs, matted and framed, each one of them bearing the same image, and when you looked at the ensemble from a distance, it formed an upside down star. By far, this was the most intriguing of all the displays, and Nena and I stared at it for a good five minutes. I questioned whether she was thinking the same thing I was, internally.

When we exited, Johnny said, "How about that camel? Pretty nice legs, huh?"

The two women found humor in the statement. I was still considering the photograph montage.

"Hey Nena, where's the bar anyway?" I asked. I felt like a drink before we observed any more art.

"It's right around the corner, if I have my bearings in order."

As we turned the corner, Nena seemed pleasantly surprised that there was a bar at the end of the block. It was then that we all realized Nena had never known exactly where Rollos was to begin with, although I did sincerely believe she frequented the place back when she came ten years ago. She probably frequented it so much that is what the cause of her blurred memory was. It could have been a bar in the Bronx for all she knew. I laughed to myself.

"There it is, but it looks like they've changed the name…" Nena said.

A laugh made it to my face. She was funny.

Johnny said, "It looks like its called The Corner Bar now." Maybe he didn't have the same realization I did. Man, he was awful dense sometimes.

"Not very creative, is it?" He added.

"Who cares, let's just get a drink." Ella said.

"That's right." I said.

"Nena, you're quite the guide I tell ya…quite the guide…" Johnny kissed her on the cheek. "Now lets get nice and polluted before we go look at any more camels with women's legs."

The four of us laughed before we entered The Corner Bar.

Chapter 13

Four windowpanes with cheap yellow curtains drawn halfway across were all that graced the right of The Corner Bar's entrance as we passed through the door. The bar was all to the left. Inadequate seating provided for a maximum capacity of sixteen to eat or drink at café tables. The rosewood bar, noticeably restored and improved, stretched almost one whole length of the establishment providing just as much seating as the café tables. There was a three-foot space between the right edge of the bar and the four windowpanes, and another three-foot space between the left edge and the unisex restroom. Also, through this same section and behind the bar was a door leading to the kitchen and receiving area. There were two patrons, an old man and an old woman, presumably a couple, sitting at the left edge of the bar near the end of it. There was no one sitting at the café tables. Lunch hour was long over and the lag time between that and happy hour was what we were currently in. I greeted the feeling of looseness, in such a tight space, fervently. The old couple didn't even look at us as we walked in.

"Welcome." The bartender had a white dishtowel slung over

his left shoulder. He wore a dirty red apron around his waist. His voice sounded cut from a crude manner, as his greeting seemed insincere and obligatory.

"Drinks?" He added. His stubbly beard was hiding something, I thought.

Before any of us had a chance to order, the old man to the left of us looked over and interjected "May I suggest the Bloody Mary...the infamous Bloody Mary made by the hand of mister Julius J. Julius there...the best bartender in all of New York..."

"Or at least in the only district of the city that is proud to bear genuine, true people." The old lady added.

Julius J. Julius, the bartender, smiled tobacco stained teeth at the couple and then took a bow. He looked back over at us, and with a crooked smirk said, "They know you're tourist."

"It's practically written all over your faces!" The old man shouted.

Julius J. Julius nodded his head in agreement.

The four of us looked back and forth at one another and struggled to contain ourselves. "We come from Denver, the home of The Rocky Mountains." Johnny said as he held the old couple's attention.

"I visited a little place called Estes Park once, a very long time ago...I must have been eighteen or so...very long time ago."

The old lady chuckled and kissed the old man on the cheek after he said that. "You better order them a drink old fool, it's the least you can do if you're about to do what I think you're about to do."

"What's that?'

"Go into one of your long-winded stories."

"Long-winded! This one isn't long-winded...Julius J. Julius get those tourists over there a round of your infamous Bloody

Mary's."

"You got it." The bartender replied. He began to prepare the drinks as the old man continued.

I looked over at my friends. The old man, his old lady friend, Julius J. Julius, and The Corner Bar had remarkably captivated us. We couldn't have dreamed of a better beginning to our journey here in New York.

"I ventured out there with a fellow bohemian friend of mine. It was a great time in our country. We were between wars, people were recovering from the depression, and I was pursuing my dream of becoming a painter. You all are too young to appreciate that time, no doubt, but it was a glorious time I tell you…just glorious.

My friend and I had just finished high school and we decided to travel cross-country by way of the Union Pacific…from New York to San Francisco. I don't remember how, or why we stopped in Colorado. I was a pretty heavy drinker back then…prohibition had just ended, that was another thing, not like it ever really made much difference to anybody, but that was just another part of the gloriousness of the time I am referring to…"

"Back then!" The old lady jibed. "What about now? Here it is, almost four o'clock in the afternoon on a Friday, and what are you doing? Drinking! Think of it, a man your age…think of it."

"Listen here you old hag, I don't see anyone putting a gun to your head…now, are you going to let me continue telling these fine people my story, or not?"

"I suppose."

Then, the old lady leaned over and whispered in our direction, "He does have a point" and threw back the rest of her drink.

Julius J. Julius interrupted his task of preparing our Bloody

Mary's to refill the old lady's glass promptly. She drank scotch, neat.

"It doesn't matter how or why we ended up there. All that matters is that we ended up there…"

The old lady picked her right hand up and down towards her mouth, simulating someone drinking too much. This caused even more outbursts, and to our delight, Julius J. Julius joined in on the glee.

"Damn it woman! Are you going to let me tell the story or not?"

Appropriately, the old lady hid a smile and let her partner continue.

"My friend and I met these two veterans from the first World War getting all up in it at a bar in Colorado Springs…what was the name of that bar, oh hell…anyhow, we met these two chaps in this Jazz bar…real sulky place, I do remember that, certainly didn't mirror the mood of the times, no sir…certainly not.

We told these two men that we were artists and that we were in search of our muse. We told them that we were traveling cross-country from New York by way of the Union Pacific, and that somehow we ended up there. They mocked us at first…we were very young…but then, when they realized we were serious they informed us of this beautiful country just three hours from where we were at named Estes Park. They told us that it would be a sufficient place to help a struggling, or aspiring, artist find his inspiration. And with that, my old chum and I headed north from Colorado Springs to Estes Park.

When we got there, we realized those two men were not lying to us…not at all. Some of the most beautiful landscape I had ever seen laid before me, and to this day I could still say that. I'm not sure if I found my true inspiration there, but it did give me the premise for my first painting. The painting was of a mountain lion's reflection in the moon on a crystal clear starry night. One of my favorite paintings I have ever done, actually..." The old man sat back and reflected as the old lady smiled and wrapped her left arm around him.

Julius J. Julius had just finished making the drinks. His face still seemed to be hiding something.

"I'm glad you four came in here today. You see, Julius J Julius, there's always a reason...always! Thank you friends for granting me that trip down memory lane. Truly appreciated...truly."

Julius J. Julius nodded to the old man as he handed the drinks off to each one of us. Collectively, the four of us held our drinks up and toasted the old couple. It was the best drink any one of us had ever tasted.

"You're right sir, that is the best Bloody Mary I have ever tasted." I said.

"You see, my man Julius J. Julius never disappoints...I'm glad you like it."

"Thank you." We all responded.

Then, Nena stood up and walked over to the old man. She carried her drink with her, in her right hand. The couple watched her with unmoving interest, and so did Julius J. Julius. Johnny, myself, and Ella were pretty darn intrigued in what she was doing as well.

Without speaking a word to the couple, or anybody else, Nena broke out into one of her jazz numbers. It was one of the harshest sounding tunes I had ever heard. Paradoxically, it was one of the most beautiful tunes I had ever heard. It was perfect. It was great. It was true.

I turned to Ella and whispered, "Is this what you mean by Drifting?"

She smiled and said, "Exactly what I mean. But wait, it'll get even better."

Nena's song was about a woman drawing inside of a telephone booth while she waited for a date that never arrived. When she was finished, the old man stood up directly in front of her. The rest of us clapped.

The old man kissed her on the cheek and said, "Thank you..." Then, he grabbed the old lady off of her stool and said, "Let's leave, I've got to go paint."

As the two headed out The Corner Bar, the old man turned around and said, "They might not be tourists after all Julius J. Julius...put whatever these four want on my tab...all night if they so desire."

"You got it." Julius J. Julius responded.

The couple disappeared into the street.

"That's Drifting." Ella said as she grabbed my arm.

I smiled and we shared a moment.

When I looked over at Johnny I noticed he was looking out the window to see where the couple was going as they walked off. When he turned back around he asked Julius J. Julius whom the old man was.

In a plainly flat voice, Julius J. Julius said, "Just an artist, like all of us."

Chapter 14

We were well into it when the black phone next to the cash register rang for the first time since we had arrived. After three rounds of Julius J. Julius' infamous Bloody Mary's, each one of us had switched over to our drink of preference. I was drinking vodka on the rocks. The bar was jammed tight now, and the sun was beginning to set outside. Even from the limiting view I had sitting at the corner barstool inside this unique establishment, the effect of the sun setting over New York sent shivers up and down my spine. We had gone almost a whole day without incident, but the night was still young, and I had a creeping sensation (one always had a creeping sensation when Johnny Bea was his best friend, but this one was beyond the usual). Ella looked plain and drawn now, as the effects of the alcohol were taking its toll on her outward appearance. Her shell, which was very thin to start with, was beginning to fade away, and the true value of her soul was beginning to surface. It was a stunning contradiction, and I had never felt more attracted to her than now.

Johnny was busy talking to a Spanish man with a handlebar mustache, while Ella and Nena talked about jazz. Ella's sophistication was bona fide, and even Jack Daniels couldn't put a dent in that. Nena was fascinated, but more so enchanted, that Ella could carry a sensible conversation with her about her one true passion. As a matter of fact, Nena was downright daunted. She even kept reminding Ella of just how much. I just absorbed everything and tried to cling onto its beauty, like a leech.

It seemed like I had been in New York for weeks, sitting on this barstool in this aptly named corner bar for most of the time, enjoying the hell out of my life. There was only one thing missing: my Drifting mate.

Julius J. Julius had received help about an hour ago in the form of a sexy young waitress with a tight fitting top and cheap white sneakers on. The Spaniard Johnny was talking to had been trying to get her attention ever since she arrived, and he had only insignificantly succeeded. It was obvious that she preferred Johnny to the Spaniard. The Spaniard did not notice this, but Johnny and I did. After Julius J. Julius picked up the phone, he called Nena over.

With complete surprise, Nena said, "Me?"

Julius J. Julius nodded his head with a smile as Nena parted the crowd and made her way around the bar to answer the call. She was out of earshot while talking on the phone, but when she returned, only Ella's curiosity outmatched mine. Johnny seemed to be oblivious to the fact that Nena had just received a phone call in a corner bar in New York City. He was still busy carousing with the Spaniard. No doubt they were drooling over the waitress with the tight top and cheap white sneakers. It was obvious innocence wasn't even part of the waitresses vocabulary, even someone like Johnny could understand that. Disrespectful son-of-a-bitch.

Ella seemed not to mind though, or at least pretend not to mind, or know any better, for the masking of the Spaniard and subsequent conversation with Johnny was adequate. And a sufficiently justifiable diversion at that. The truth hid beyond her eyes in the depths of her heart, though.

Nena had one of those expressions like she couldn't believe the good fortune that had just come her way.

"What? What is it? Who was that?" Ella wasn't even sure why she was excited, but she knew Nena was, therefore she felt she needed to be. She was a true friend to those she kept close.

"Yeah, what was that all about?" I felt some excitement in the air as well. The effect women have.

Nena shook her head back and forth a few times. I'm not sure if she was trying to shake her thoughts to an instance of sobriety, or if she was shaking them to belief…or both.

"The old man who has so generously allowed us to drink on his tab…"

"Yes of course. How could we forget him? He was divine." Ella interrupted. She was truly excited.

"What did he say?" I didn't prompt myself to speak, but the words just came out.

"He told me that he was happy to find that we were still here, enjoying ourselves…at least he assumed we were enjoying ourselves. Then, he asked how long we had been in town. I told him we just arrived earlier this afternoon and that Soho was the first place we visited. I told him that we went to a few galleries and then felt like having a drink. And that's when, and why, we ended up here…"

"Yeah!" Ella said.

"The old man began to laugh on the other end. He was laughing with joy, or even pride, it seemed. Then, he told me that he knew his money would be well spent on us and that we could stay at the bar as long as we'd like, drinking on his tab…"

"Yeah!" Ella and I said simultaneously this time. Once

again, I didn't remember prompting myself to speak. We looked over at one another and smiled out of mutual consideration. Ella brushed my thigh with her delicate hand.

"What a guy. I wonder who he was…or is." Ella said as she refocused back on Nena. I was disappointed she could return to normalcy so quickly after such a touch. I festered over that as Nena continued.

"I thanked him continuously until he cut me off and said, 'But I think I know a place that you might enjoy even better…if you are so inclined.' I told him we were so inclined… or at least that I was. I said, 'Oh yeah.' And he responded with 'Oh yeah.' And then he started to laugh again. I laughed as well. Then, he said, 'Miss, you sure inspired me, and the fact that you and your group has come to New York and the first thing you did was come to our little bohemian district here and belly up with Julius J. Julius tells me that you guys are real and that none of you are artificial. The reason I offered you guys to drink on my tab was because of your singing, but now, since you tell me that you didn't go straight to Lady Liberty or take a tour down Fifth Avenue in hopes of catching a glimpse of a star or some nonsense like that, and since I know all of you are real, I am not only proud to be living in the same country as you all, but I am privileged. Therefore, I am privileged to tell you that I have an old friend who plays over at the café in The Drake. I've known him for years. The old lady and I go see him as often as we can, whenever he's in town. He's terrific, and I know his music is right up your alley…it's the only café in New York that's worth its salt. If you and your group are so inclined to go see my friend, I have reserved the table right in front of his piano for you all. And, don't worry about the drink minimum, that's taken care of…although judging by the way you real people are, I don't think that'll be a problem. But, if for some reason you are displeased with the music, don't worry about the drink minimum…'" Nena paused to catch her breath and take a drink. Ella and I did the same.

"Then he informed me that his friends name was BoJo, and that the table was reserved for the Estes party. I thanked him countless times again, and he said that was unnecessary. He told me BoJo went on at ten. I told him we would be there."

"What an incredibly amazing person." Ella said. Then, she turned around to me and added, "And my parents always said New Yorkers were haughty and pompous…where are those people?"

I toasted her and nodded my head.

Nena continued, "Wait, it gets better, check this out, as we were hanging up the phone the old man says 'Oh yeah, by the way, old BoJo might be looking for a partner.' Then he hung up…"

Nena paused to catch her breath. She took another drink. Ella and I waited.

"A partner? What do you guys think about that? Do you think he's serious?" It was only normal for Nena's instinct to question the ensuing good graces that were possibly awaiting her.

Sure the old man was serious. He was no liar. He was real.

"Why would he be lying Nena?" I stated in defense of the old man. I found her comment upsetting, even though I understood where it originated.

"It is rather amazing…but, guess what? We're going to find out, that's for sure." Ella said as she stood up and gave Nena a heartfelt, genuine hug.

"This is too good." Nena added as the two women embraced tightly.

"What time is it?" Nena asked nervously as reality set in.

Julius J. Julius was standing behind the bar, mysteriously. His face was still inconspicuous. He was listening to our whole conversation. "It is nine o'clock right now. The Drake is in the upper side. You guys better finish up and get going. Traffic is pretty hectic on Friday nights."

Finally, Johnny turned away from the Spaniard and back over to us. "What's up? I overheard something about a café."

"The old man…you know the one who is paying for our drinks…has reserved a table for us over at the café in The Drake Hotel. Apparently, he's tight with the piano player, BoJo, and has some pull." I responded.

"And, he also said that BoJo might be looking for a partner." Ella added. Nena looked down at the floor in slight embarrassment and even slighter pride.

"What kind of partner?"

Johnny was so damn dense! It was always made worse after he'd been drinking.

"What kind of partner? Johnny, what do you think? A crooning partner." Ella's antipathy wasn't just limited to this current dealing with her man. It had finally become apparent to her that Johnny was thick, and it was gnawing away at her patience with each passing moment.

"Hell, I don't know. I was thinking something else…I don't know, Damn it!"

"Calm down Johnny…" I stated boldly.

Immediately Johnny held my eyes with a look that could have stopped a clock. He had never given me that look before. I had seen him present it to others, but never me. It horrified me terribly, and I envisioned tumult ahead if I did not cower and avert my eyes appropriately. The alcohol was giving me a sense of courage, though, so I stared right back at him, poignantly. He wasn't expecting that.

"God Damn it Emerson, watch it!"

Ella jumped in. The tension between us had arrived and escalated in not a moments notice, and she didn't want it to come to a head. How could she have known these feelings had rankled long before tonight?

Boy, was I feeling it.

Right now, I didn't care if the head burst wide open...and I believed Johnny preferred it. I was sick of his attitude. I thought of Ella's comment a moment ago about what her parents thought of New Yorkers. If anyone around here was haughty and pompous, it was Johnny...from the Midwest.

"Come on Johnny, relax. You two are the greatest of friends for crying out loud. Let's all be excited about this, together as friends. This is what we came for...isn't it Johnny? To experience New York. The old man saw that, he appreciated it, and he has rewarded us for it. Please, for my sake, for Nena's sake, for the old man's sake, don't get crazy on me...that goes for you too Emerson...both of you relax, now! I am not going to let anyone ruin this for us, and certainly not either one of you two...I don't care if you are my friends. You won't be for the remainder of this trip if you continue on with this type of behavior...acting like a couple of adolescent schoolboys...ridiculous I tell you."

The only part of Ella's spiel I caught was the reference to friends. It was encouraging to know that she didn't refer to Johnny as her man, or single him out in any way.

I remained silent, eyes locked hard on Johnny.

I felt as if I had just been caught up in a whirlwind, and then wickedly released. Things changed in that instant.

Johnny shrugged and turned back around to the Spaniard.

After he did that, I apologized to Nena and Ella. Johnny did not.

"We'll finish these drinks and get going...okay Johnny?" It was more of a statement than a question, but Johnny turned around. He drew his silence out before he nodded his head to Ella.

His insolence was starting to get under her skin too. Nena didn't seem to care, she had more important matters to concern herself with: BoJo and the café.

Disturbing thoughts ran ramped in the back of my mind, inching their way closer and closer to the front with each passing second. But I allowed decency and common courtesy from the soul to push forth, beyond those thoughts.

"The alcohol must be hitting me stiffer than usual…hey Johnny, I'm sorry."

Johnny turned all the way around from the Spaniard. He nodded instinctively and said, "Me too."

I questioned his authenticity.

"Good, now that we got that cleared up and out of the way, and now that you two are back to your old ways, we can all get back to being normal." Ella said with a smile. It was a hopeful smile.

I knew nothing would be normal ever again.

Chapter 15

I had never been inside a hotel that was so elegantly European. Usually, I associate European décor with gaudiness. Perhaps, another tell that I am not well traveled. The lobby boasted modishness but with a subtly luxurious tribute to tradition. The service was exceptional, as I expected.

The bellhop held the door open for each of us and greeted us with an offer of assistance as we passed by. "No thanks" we said as a group. "We're here to see BoJo at the café."

"You all are in for quite a treat...best cabaret performer in New York City...when he's here of course...enjoy." The bellhop said. "Just follow the people, and you'll find the café no problem."

Johnny led our group and I brought up the rear with Nena. There was two or three foot of distance between Johnny and Ella as they walked. Either he was still fumed, or she was; I presumed the former.

The smell of cigar smoke, pipe smoke, and cigarette smoke was what hit me first. No one had a coat to check, but the attendants offered anyways. I didn't understand. There was a line that we were able to circumvent by way of Johnny's brashness and formidable presence. Immediately, I felt ashamed by the sets of eyes running up and down us as Johnny told the host "Estes party."

"Right this way sir."

The host led us through the smoke-filled, dimly lit room. I wondered if it was always this smoky and dark. A sense of undeniable awareness washed over me before the four of us sat down. That feeling was instantly stripped away from me when Johnny made a crack about how dark it was. He was very drunk.

BoJo was preparing for the beginning of his set. His piano lay directly in front of us. I picked up on the fact that eyes were still running over us; this was discernible even with the lack of light. BoJo wore a black suit with a black tie. It matched the color of his spongy hair and lip whiskers. His teeth were as bright as the snow and they were ever-present, for he smiled constantly.

BoJo nodded to us as we took our seats. He made it a point to the host to make sure we were afforded anything we desired with a simple nod of his head. The host took our drink orders and then retreated. Two minutes later our drinks were at the table.

The only people in the surrounding area I could make out were a middle-aged couple behind our table. They were very cosmopolitan. The man was prettier than the woman. I smiled at the two as they returned the favor. Then, the place fell silent, so silent, it was menacing.

I had never been in a place so quiet and so dark at the same time. The café couldn't possibly be like this every night. That would be too good to be fact. But, then again, fiction is nowhere to be found in New York. I desperately wanted to hold onto this place…forever.

As BoJo tickled the keys and amplified a combination of

some of the most harmonious chords I had ever imagined a lounge piano player capable of striking, I thought of my favorite pianist, Rachmaninoff. Although the obvious difference in musical style and in talent was observable and evident, the music BoJo played gave me the same sensation that Rachmaninoff's did: comfort and peace. It was inexplicable in its brilliancy. I loved New York.

After his first set, which lasted about twenty minutes, BoJo took a break. The lights came on and the smatterings of delicately restrained conversation resumed. I turned and noticed the sophisticated couple behind us leaving. I watched the host seat two goliaths for men. They both wore blue jeans and a sports blazer. Underneath the blazers, both men wore a tight fitting gray shirt. The shirts read MARINES. They looked like marines. It pleased me to see them there. I had never before likened our services, much less those who are part of the marines service, to appreciation of good jazz. It was peacetime though, so one can never tell. I was curious as to why they had their civilian clothes on and not their uniforms. I asked them. They told me they were on weekend leave, and that they preferred to wear their casuals while on leave. Then, I asked them why they wore the tee-shirts bearing the name of MARINES on it. Both of them responded by saying, "You can't deny a man his true nature." I laughed and we toasted together. They went about their business as I returned to the table.

BoJo was talking to Nena. She was flirting with him, absurdly and obscenely. He was eating it up. I reckoned they were about the same age as one another. They were actually cute in their repulsive demeanor.

"Our mutual friend tells me you like jazz." BoJo said as he took her hand. He even had the ability to speak through his smile.

"Yes sir..."

"Honeydrop, don't call me sir, please. You say sir and I look around for my granddaddy." BoJo successfully elicited a round of laughter from everybody...everybody except Johnny. "Are you a singer?"

"Yes BoJo, but nowhere near the likes of you."

"I doubt that...I'll tell you what, if you have a drink with me after this next set, why don't I hand the mike over to you for a song or two."

"Are you serious?"

"Always, Honeydrop."

I found difficulty in believing that last statement because of his permanent smile, but Nena didn't, and that was all that mattered.

"I would be honored."

"So would I."

"Wonderful."

"I've got to go back to the ivory now, but you all enjoy your drinks...and I'll see you, Honeydrop, in about thirty." BoJo was interested only in Nena. The rest of us might as well not have even been at the table, or existed for that matter. BoJo wasn't rude or disrespectful about it, he was just being who he was...he was being true. And the rest of us understood that, except Johnny.

"Why didn't he even introduce himself to us? I mean, the least someone can do is acknowledge the presence of others." Johnny said. He was terribly drunk.

"Oh Johnny." Ella was cautious with her tongue. She now completely understood that Johnny could lose it at any second.

I kept silent. This could be the crucial advantage I was looking for.

What was I talking about?

Johnny shrugged and stared at BoJo roughly, as if he

couldn't believe some lounge singer (which was all Johnny saw him as, not an artist or musician, just a dull lounge singer…he was so damn thick) had the gall to treat him with such disrespect. BoJo just smiled and prepared himself for the next set as if he didn't even notice. And he didn't, or at least he didn't care.

"That really gets me, man. Damn it!" Johnny said boisterously.

Those at the tables around us stared. I slouched in my seat out of mortification. I was mulling over what it was I liked about Johnny, and I had trouble coming up with anything relevant.

Ella leaned over and smacked Johnny on the knee.

"What? What the hell did you do that for? All I'm looking for is a little respect. A little common courtesy extended from one man to another."

"Keep it down Johnny, people are staring. Don't ruin this for Nena. I don't care about me, but don't you dare ruin this for her…keep it down!" Ella whispered as best she could. Poor girl.

Johnny didn't even give her the decency of a glance. He slammed his drink and said, "Go to hell!"

Ella was stunned senseless with disbelief. Tears initialized in her magnificent eyes as she quickly found, and retreated to, her drink. She wiped the drops from her eyes with class, and then turned to Nena and said, "You're going to be divine Nena, divine I tell you." Ella was more elegant than any damn hotel could ever be.

Nena smiled at her.

I had never been so humiliated.

"Hey listen man, I don't know who you think you are, talking to your woman like that and disrespecting BoJo like you are, but you better keep a lid on it." One of the gigantic marines had his left hand on Johnny's shoulder. He had leaned around me to get to him.

I believe Johnny was as stunned by what he heard as his girl was just moments before. That only dazed him for seconds though, literally.

Johnny smiled at the man confidently…arrogantly. His cold stare penetrated the marine's dark eyes. "I know who I am. Unfortunately, for your sake, you don't. Since this is a cabaret and not a roadhouse bar, I'm going to do something I normally don't do and ask you politely to remove your hand from my shoulder. I don't prefer to cause a scene, but it's happened many times before, and I'm not opposed if you're willing. But think hard, I certainly don't want you or your jarhead pal to have to be on leave for longer than you already are…medical leave is what I'm referring to."

I had witnessed Johnny take on two, three, four, and even five guys before, but none were even close to the size of these two…not even combined. Yet, even with this, I knew Johnny was more convinced than ever that he could pulverize these marines.

It just dawned on me that I no longer desired to watch Johnny fight, in any venue or in any form. Actually, just the idea of it sickened me.

I figured the marines were more sensible and mature than Johnny, but their laughter made me unsure. "Hey Chance, get a hold of this guy…did you hear that?"

The marine that spoke had turned around to his friend, Chance. He did remove his hand from Johnny's shoulder, though, before he did so. The friend, still seated at the table, shook his head in disbelief. I slouched even further in my seat.

The beginning of BoJo's set broke the uneasy and intense silence. The lights fell, and the marines awaited a response.

Before Johnny could react, Ella leaned into him and said,

"If you dare try one thing…one goddamn thing…I swear I will never speak to you again."

I looked over at Nena. She was almost in tears.

Johnny chewed over his options for a moment and wisely chose to remain seated. He ordered another drink from the waitress with a flick of his wrist and forgot about the marine standing over him for the time being.

The marine reassumed his previous position. "Smart kid." He said.

Johnny refocused on BoJo as Ella privileged herself to a sigh of relief. Nena gathered herself together, before any drops fell. I wasn't sure if she was emotional because of Johnny or because of her nerves, but she really wasn't the type that would let someone like Johnny Bea cause her internal distress or cause her to ruin her chances…at anything. It must have been her nerves.

A feeling of dissention had cast itself over the table like an honest blanket. BoJo's music wasn't as pleasing to the ears, and soul, as it was during the first set. I became conscious of myself staring at Ella desperately, without regard for Johnny. She was staring back at me.

When BoJo's second set ended Ella excused herself to go to the bathroom. I watched her all the way out. As I retracted my vision to the table I noticed the two marines had seemed to have forgotten about the incident during the first intermission. As I turned back around, BoJo was beckoning the host over to him. He whispered something to the host and then pointed at Nena. When the host returned, he handed BoJo two snifters filled halfway with brandy. BoJo ambled over with his glowing smile and sat down where Ella had been sitting. Nena and him shared a drink and then became entranced by one another.

Johnny got up from the table.

I watched him make his way over to the marines. He

obviously saw an opening while Ella was gone; his logic was confined by his inherently punchy nature. Did he really think he could start and finish something without her knowing?

The two marines were surprised, to put it lightly, when Johnny interrupted them by sticking his baldhead in between their space and placing his arms around them. "How about we finish what we started boys? Meet me outside, in front…that is if you two really are as tough as you think you are…" Then he smiled and flipped the one named Chance's ear with his index finger. "What do you say, Chance?"

The two marines sat silently bewildered as Johnny strutted out of the room. When they realized the call that had just transpired before their very eyes, they made no hesitation. The two marines followed Johnny out.

I waited for Ella to return. This was an opportunity.

"Where's Johnny?" She asked with minimal concern when she returned to the table.

Nena and BoJo were still lost in one another. They could have cared less about Johnny. I fully agreed with them.

I didn't say a word.

Ella lowered her shoulders. She refused to believe the truth when she realized the two marines behind us were missing, and another couple had taken place in their stead.

"Sit down Ella. Don't worry about it. Don't even think about it. Just sit down and drink with me. You don't deserve the treatment he lashes you with…you don't, and you know it! You're too good for him. You're too good for that. Here, sit down and drink with me."

Ella sat, but she didn't drink. Instead, she buried her head in my shoulder. I gripped her strongly with my right arm…never wishing the moment to cease. When the third set commenced, Ella and I were still in the same position. I truly loved her.

Johnny, nor the marines, had returned, but everything was

fine according to me. BoJo was introducing Nena to the crowd as Ella popped up and said, "Emerson, will you please go find him?"

I didn't understand.

There was only one thing to do.

I kissed her on the cheek and said "Sure."

On the walk back to the lobby my thoughts were consumed by nothing but passionate illustrations of Ella and I. I did not harbor any ill feelings or remorse about them either. In fact, I appreciated them.

The bellhop was not there to open the door for me. I saw him outside. He was leaning down. When I arrived outside on the sidewalk, I saw the two marines. Both were unconscious and severely beaten. There was blood, but not as much as one would think from the look of their faces. Oddly, a crowd had not assembled...must have just been another scene in New York for the natives who were passing by during the brawl.

"What happened?" I asked the bellhop.

I knew the bellhop recognized me from earlier. He knew I was with Johnny. I actually hoped he had not remembered, though, for I was no longer willing to claim Johnny as a friend.

"Your pal! Your pal is what happened! I've never seen such stupidity befall one man. He's crazy! He's fucking crazy!" The bellhop exclaimed, and then returned his attention to the wounded men. "The ambulance is on its way."

"Ambulance? They're still breathing aren't they?" Stupid question.

"Yeah, of course, but just look at them, they obviously need a doctor."

"Where did my pal, Johnny, happen to go? Did you see?" I did regret using Johnny's name, but the bellhop was too preoccupied with the marines to notice.

"He just ran off...just took off down the street, running.

Drift

Son-of-a-bitch!"

"Which way? Where was he going?"

"How the hell am I supposed to know? He just took off, running. The Son-of-a-bitch!"

When I returned to the café, reluctance was written all over my face, I could feel it. I was happy to find the crowd standing in applause. I realized it was for Nena. Ella was hugging her when I arrived back at the table. Everyone was focused on the two. The noise recoiled and BoJo returned gracefully to his ivory. Nena had begun to tell Ella something. She was frightfully excited.

I sat down. Ella turned to me. She had a wide smile on her face. She was caught up in Nena's splendor. "Emerson, you missed it, Nena was incredible. I've never seen anything like it. She was divine."

I looked across at Nena who had just found her seat. She was so ecstatic her smile could not be contained. I forced a grin.

"I'm sorry I missed it Nena, truly, but I always thought you were amazing, and now everybody else does too…I knew it when I first met you, truly."

"Yeah, and listen to this…BoJo wants her to stay."

"The night?"

"No. For good. In New York." Ella concluded.

Now, my happiness was not compulsory. I was honestly pleased for Nena. This was her calling. I leaned over and hugged her. The two of us didn't even say a word. We had a mutual understanding.

"You're a great person Emerson parks. A true spirit. Don't let anyone ever tell you any different." Nena told me.

We embraced again. I felt like weeping.

"Where's Johnny?" Ella asked.

I looked up at the ceiling, and then located my drink on the

table and finished it off.
"Gone."

Chapter 16

It was easier for Ella to blame the city than Johnny. She kept repeating 'Even someone like Johnny can get lost in a place like this.' And she didn't mean lost in the physical sense. I was nothing short of astounded about her outlook on the situation. I was even more perturbed when her persona took on one of diffidence. Perhaps she too was lost. I feared she thought...or worse yet desired...Johnny to be her Drifting mate. I was thoroughly disheartened.

I was upset with Johnny. But now, back in his hotel room with his girl, I couldn't remember why. All I could focus on was how Ella seemed to lose all esteem for herself the second I told her Johnny was gone. It was a mind-numbing comprehension. It just made me even more mad about her. Ironically, I sometimes felt the exact same way she was feeling, and it was satisfying to find someone sharing the same affliction...which is precisely what it was.

After Bojo's final set was finished, Johnny had not reappeared (so why should either one of us have thought he was going to come back to The Drake? I knew he would not, but Ella insisted that we stay there a while just in case). During that time, Ella and I saw Nena off over fifteen minutes worth of tears. Nena had really affected us, and both Ella and I were better off for knowing her for the brief period we had. BoJo would be affected by her in the same way, and probably even deeper. They both deserved it, because they were both tremendously real people. Ella and I did not say much on the way back to our hotel, except for the constant reminders of how Johnny's disappearance was the city's fault. It was actually quite irritating, for I believed the best thing that has ever happened to me has taken place in this city, on this trip, during these past ten to twelve hours, but I wasn't going to let Ella know that. It was my time to be sympathetic and understanding, which I was.

We sat together on the double bed in the hotel room. The world around us seemed silent and empty, yet fully contained within the walls of this majestic city. And to think, we were smack dab in the middle of it. Anxiety danced through my blood, and I noticed my heart drastically increase in pace.

Ella lied down and put her head in my lap.

I stroked her gorgeous locks gently. "Maybe we should just drift right on out of here. No one will have to know. Just get up and leave this place...no worries whatsoever. Slide right out the door and drift away into the New York night. Just you and I." I didn't remember those thoughts coming to my head. It was like before, only these thoughts were much more important. I couldn't control my tongue. Instantly, I sobered up.

With mounting dread, I awaited a response. When I didn't receive one, I delicately placed Ella's hair back behind her ear and then moved my pursed lips along her sleek jaw-line. I was no longer in control.

It was like nothing previously experienced. I felt like I was floating. When my lips touched hers, heaven knocked on the door. The last thing on my mind was Johnny, or where he happened to be.

I had never tasted such pain and pleasure before. I could not differentiate between exhilaration and horrification. But, for that moment...that definitive moment...I did not care a bit about the consequences when it was all over.

Unfortunately, I knew that it would be over, and that it would not last forever. Just like everything that was good in this world. Nothing ever lasts. Nothing.

Ella struggled to unlock her lips from mine, but her principles overshadowed her emotions this round. "This is wrong. We can't do this."

"Why not? I don't know what it is exactly that I am feeling, but I can tell you that it definitely doesn't feel wrong...I don't believe it is wrong."

"Yes you do. You've got to. You're the strong one Emerson, not me...we've got to go find Johnny."

My shoulders fell to the burden of my head-strength, and I fell back against the bed. Something had just come crashing down on me...truth and reality. I thought back to the time Johnny referred to me as an idealist, just like my parents. I wished I were. "What about existentialism, and Drifting, and all that?"

I shouldn't have asked the question. I regretted it before I even finished asking it. I knew I could not handle the responses I dismayed. I had faith in Ella, and everything she stood for, and I did not want that to be destroyed along with everything else. It was too fragile. I was too fragile.

"Finding Johnny is only about finding Johnny, it's not about anything else. Obviously, a lot has changed since we arrived in this town, a hell of a lot. Nothing will ever be normal or the same between Johnny and I...or you and I for that matter."

Underneath my breath I murmured, "Don't forget Johnny and I."

She did not hear me, thankfully.

"But that doesn't mean he's not still our friend, right? We can't just leave him…"

"Don't say another word. Let's go."

Her comments, and where I thought they might have been leading, gave me that sinking sensation I feared, and I just could not listen to any more. I was losing faith in her…in everything.

As we flagged down a cab, Ella asked, "Where should we start?"

"My guess…which would be my only guess…is The Corner Bar. If he's not there, then we'll never be able to find him…do you understand how big this city is?"

"Yes, I know Emerson."

That was the first time Ella had ever been short with me. I didn't know what was happening, or how much more of it I could stand.

We told the cabbie to take us to The Corner Bar in Soho, and, amazingly, he knew where it was.

The Corner Bar had not lost any steam; in fact it had gained some. There wasn't a line at the door, but you could tell from the street corner it was standing room only. Ella and I peered in through the window, beyond the half-drawn curtains that covered it. Through the heavy crowd I was able to recognize a familiar face. It was the Spaniard. He was sitting at one of the café tables now. There was somebody sitting across from him. It was the sexy waitress. Her shift must have ended, because I spotted another waitress, not nearly as sexy, battling the crowd with a tray full of drinks. I looked back at the Spaniard and waitress. They were laughing and having a good time. I thought of how drunk the Spaniard must be.

Then, I noticed an empty chair next to the waitress. My anxiety might as well never have subsided. I looked over at

Ella. "Is he in there?" I asked her, but I already knew the answer.

"I don't know. It's hard to get a good view of everything from this vantage point."

"I don't see him. Maybe we should go."

"Hold on, Emerson. We've only been here a few minutes. Just give me a couple more."

"Come on Ella, he's not in there…" I returned my attention to the inside. Johnny was coming out of the restroom. It was easy to pick up on his baldness through the sea of people. He was headed towards the Spaniard and the waitress. "Let's get out of here, Ella. I don't see him."

"Yes you do, Emerson. So do I."

I closed my eyes. When I reopened them Johnny was kissing the sexy waitress. After a few minutes, they released and took a shot together along with the Spaniard. I closed my eyes again. I did not want to bear witness any longer, for I had never seen Johnny so happy.

Ella did not weep or anything. I think she rather expected what she saw. She knew Johnny better than I thought she did. I offered her my arm, but she did not accept it.

I felt numb.

"Let's go."

We walked all the way back to the hotel.

Chapter 17

Ella had a fifth of Jack Daniels stashed away in her bag for just such an occasion. Possibly, she anticipated such events. The long walk back to the hotel had sufficed in sobering her up...I sobered up before we even left to seek out Johnny...but neither one of us was tired. The whiskey was indeed welcomed.

Ella had removed her shoes, and so had I. This served as an adequate tension reliever. This time, the two of us sat in the putrid chairs adorning the coffee table in the room. Both of us rested our feet on the top as we passed the bottle back and forth.

"That idea about us Drifting off together doesn't sound so bad right about now, does it?" I said whimsically. I wanted a response though.

Ella laughed. I joined her.

"You know what's funny, Emerson? The fact that I have always considered myself a strong-willed and strong principled person...I pride myself on those attributes!"

I sensed uneasiness about Ella, as if something other than Johnny and the whole night in New York City was weighing on her conscience...something beyond. "Why is that funny?"

"Because the truth of the matter is I'm neither one of those things. I'm not real…I'm a fraud."

"Don't go talking like that. I've never met anyone anywhere near your authenticity, Ella. You are those attributes you spoke of, and a whole lot more. I would be lying to you if I didn't tell you I was envious of you. So much so it pains me sometimes."

She smiled and took a pull off the bottle. "One quality I do know for sure that I still possess is keen intuition…"

We both laughed. That comment was humorous, but off the mark. My intentions in my remarks were not undercoated with sexual desires. I meant what I told her. "Sincerely Ella, I'm serious. I would not lie to you, ever."

"Thank you."

I lit myself a cigarette and then lit one for her.

"This is a strange city." She said offhand.

"I think it's spectacular…the best city I have ever been privileged to visit."

She looked at me sideways. "It's foreboding, Emerson."

"It's forlornly, Ella, that's the ironic majesty of it…that's what makes it so captivating. There's something deeper, past the sense of desperation and near-hopelessness that the city appears to portray. There's a raw, real, true soul beyond that exterior, Ella. It's not foreboding…it's glorious."

"I've always believed you to be an interesting person, Emerson Parks. Always."

"What is it that Johnny always says, 'Can't deny a man his true nature,' I guess that's mine…I'm interesting. Man, is that sad. I need a drink." I took the bottle from Ella and swallowed two mouthfuls.

"It's not sad, Emerson. There are a lot worse things one can be than interesting. Look at it this way: the fact that you're interesting means that you have a bunch of different traits floating around in that body of yours, and when they come to surface it causes people great interest in you."

"People. What people? Like who?"

"Like Me."

I wasn't positive if that was an invitation and approval for advancement, or not. I was not ready to push it just yet though.

"Do you believe the reason Johnny was kissing that girl, and that you were granted witness to it, had something to do with what happened between us just before we left to go find him?"

"I don't know what I believe anymore. I knew Johnny wasn't my soulmate…my Drifting mate. I realized that last week after the incident at The Hill. He's too insecure, and he tries to compensate for it in the most asininely immature ways…"

"You don't believe his true nature is that of a street fighter? You believe he is something more?"

"I sure hope so. If not, my faith in humanity is something I will have to question…there's got to be something more to Johnny than just that. Just like there's got to be something more to you than just the fact that you're interesting…doesn't there?"

"I'm not sure."

We reflected silently, for a moment, while we smoked our cigarettes.

Had one huge trick been played upon us? Maybe this city was foreboding, and maybe it was indicative of the rest of the world?

I took another drink. "What would those Drifters say about all of this?"

"I think they would say 'Yes, that is all there is, and don't read any deeper into what your heart is telling you; a man is just a man; a woman is just a woman; take it for that and go with it. Don't think too hard and make the best of your life while you're still able to…because who knows? Maybe tomorrow you won't be around.' But that's just what I think." She finished with a drink. Then she added, "That sounds like something you would say, and believe, Emerson. Perhaps you are a Drifter."

"Are Drifters realists?" I asked.

"I believe I just determined that they are. I never looked at it in that fashion before. I never would have correlated the two before this trip, but now that I do, it makes perfect sense."

"Possibly, that is what has been holding you back? Now that the realization is upon you, you can go forward with your dreams of becoming a Drifter."

Ella thought long and hard. She finished off the bottle and said, "I think I'm too scared."

I took her hand and said, "That's why I'm here."

Ella and I transcended the world in a matter of moments as we shucked all the terrible things about it and tried to leave them behind in a wake of passion.

Next, we found ourselves holding onto one another as we welcomed slumber.

It was four thirty when Johnny finally came through the door. The noise he made startled both of us awake. What he saw was definitely not what he expected when he flipped on the lights. He was grotesquely drunk, but not so drunk that he couldn't find the ability to throw me against the wall with blunt force. My whole body agonized from the impact. He was yelling at the top of his lungs, right in my face. Spit and drool followed each expletive. I didn't understand one word he was sputtering. His face was so red it looked like his head could explode at any minute.

When he was finished with me, he turned to Ella. I started to comprehend some of the words that were coming out of his mouth when he started hurling them at her. The last thing I heard him say before he hit her was "Ungrateful whore!"

I picked the empty bottle of Jack Daniels up off of the table and broke it against the top. I rushed Johnny with it and got him right in the side, next to his kidney.

What the hell was wrong with me? What was I doing?

All I heard was piercing screams rattling in my head.

I just wanted them to stop.

There was only one thing I remember saying to myself before unconsciousness set in. 'Drift away.'

Chapter 18

When I came to my senses, I found myself alone. Unfortunately, I realized I had not just awakened from some horrible nightmare. When I looked at myself in the mirror my face was almost unrecognizable. I could hardly tolerate looking at it. As I left the room, I noticed bloodstains on the carpet from the cut I inflicted upon Johnny. I wished I had killed him.

I chose to exit the hotel by way of the fire escape. I opened the window at the end of the hallway and jumped out onto the stairs. The city didn't seem as fantastic, as majestic, as it did last night. I wasn't sure what I was going to do, but I had an overwhelming feeling that I was going to run into Johnny and Ella wherever I went.

Why did Ella go with him? Did she go with him?

We still had a whole day in New York before our flight left, but I knew there was no way I could deal with Johnny…possibly ever again…so I knew I would not be on that flight tomorrow. I had very little money, and in this town one needed money if he wanted to leave, or else it would sink its claws into you and never let go.

I found a payphone and called The Drake. I was very

paranoid. I was conscious of my eyes darting in every direction…back and forth, forth and back. Those who walked by me picked up on my paranoia. When the receptionist answered I asked her if Nena McCray had a room there. When she told me that Nena did not I then proceeded to ask her if the piano player, BoJo, had a room there. She just laughed at that one. I hung up the phone.

I walked into a gift shop and bought a cheap pair of sunglasses, a miniature model of the Statue of Liberty, and a pack of cigarettes. Everybody in the gift shop stared at me tightly, even the foreign clerk. I needed to find refuge.

After an hour and a half of walking around the city aimlessly…confused…hurting…helpless…hopeless, I found myself back in the Soho district. I recognized one of the galleries my friends and I perused through yesterday. Yesterday seemed so long ago…like an eternity. I remembered that The Corner Bar was on the next street over.

When I tried to open the door I found it locked. I walked over to the transparent windowpanes. I saw Julius J. Julius inside cleaning drink glasses behind the bar. I knocked on the windowpane glass. With more concern for his task than the person knocking on the glass, he yelled, "We don't open until eleven."

I knocked again, this time harder and louder. Julius J. Julius looked up with minor disgust. He squinted to make me out clearer. I motioned through the glass for him to let me in. He squinted again, and then placed the glass he was cleaning down on the bar and headed for the door; he stared at me the whole way. I nodded my head to assure him I was on the up and up as he tried to decipher who it was hiding behind the dark sunglasses and mangled face. I saw him unlock the door.

"What happened to you?" Julius J. Julius asked. His tone was so dry it was almost lazy.

I presumed Julius J. Julius never got frazzled or concerned with too much of anything. He saw everything how it was, and nothing more. "It's a long story..." I took my glasses off so he could see my eyes. "My friends...if I can even label them that anymore...and I were in here last night, remember? Jazz singer? We drank on that old man's tab."

"Of course I remember...your friend came in here solo last night and picked up on old Marcy...left with her too."

"Do you mind if I come in?"

Julius J. Julius allowed me entrance by way of simple gesture, and then quickly returned to his cleansing duties.

"I suppose the reason your friends are not with you has something to do with why your face looks like it does."

"Everything to do with it Julius J. Julius...everything. They all abandoned me, Julius J. Julius. It's not surprising though."

"Oh yeah?"

"Yeah. Hey, do you think I could get one of those infamous Bloody Mary's you make so well?"

"I suppose I could do that for you, as long as you assure me that they...they meaning the drinks...are not the main reason for why your luck had dramatically turned for the worst."

"I assure you, alcohol played no role in the travesty of a friendship that disassembled last night. If anything, it prolonged the inevitable."

"Alright then."

Julius J. Julius prepared the drink. I watched him closely. His secret ingredients were fresh garlic and a touch of cilantro. He slid the drink down to me after he finished making it. I handed him a five-dollar bill, and then realized I only had thirty-two left. Julius J. Julius picked the bill up off of the bar and then put it in his pocket. He wasn't just the bartender, he was the owner.

"You guys seemed like old chums last night, the four of

you...maybe with the minimal exception of the singer. But you still all looked to be very close. Why do you feel the friendships were a travesty?"

I looked at him very deliberately. He maintained interest with his ears opened to me while his eyes refocused upon his dirty drink glasses. Each time he finished one, the damp rag squeaked along the inside rims of the glass. It was very annoying, but he was just doing his job, as well as trying to help...or at least understand...a sorry soul like me. I realized, contrary to what I thought yesterday, that Julius J. Julius was not hiding anything, for he had nothing to hide. He was just a regular old chap, living a regular old life, trying to get along just like everybody else. I envied his regular existence as I took a drink off of his orangey-red concoction. This one tasted even better than the ones yesterday.

I smacked my lips and said, "The singer has nothing to do with this...she's a grand woman, a sweetheart lady. And that old man last night, that generous old coot..." After I said that I gritted my teeth in anger. That was one of Johnny's sayings.

Why the hell did that come out of my mouth?

"He set Nena up with BoJo over at The Drake, and she decided to stay in New York with him..."

"Good. The old man will be delighted to hear that."

"Who was that old man anyways?"

"Take another drink and continue your story. The singer had nothing to do with it, but what was it about your friend and the girl?"

"I thought I was in love...with the girl, but now I am not so sure. Before New York she was his...his meaning my best friend's...girl. That's just the way it was. Sure, I havened feelings for her within, strong feelings to be exact, but he was my best friend...what was I going to do?"

"Was the relationship exclusive...I mean between him and

her?"

I thought that last comment was interesting, and it made me think. I took another drink and said, "She thought it was...I assume."

"I was going to say, it certainly did not seem that way last night...at least the second time your friend was here. He and Marcy seemed pretty affectionate. Old Marcy...she has a tendency to bring the worst out in a man." Julius J. Julius looked like he was speaking from experience.

"I know. Ella...that's the girl's name...and I came back here last night trying to find him and we saw the two together."

"And that's when you thought it was a good time to make your move?"

"How long have you been a bartender, Julius J. Julius?" I laughed between drinks.

"You're right, I've certainly heard similar stories in the past, but one doesn't have to have a bent ear to figure you out."

"I'm that flat, huh? That's humorous. Ella thinks I'm interesting."

"I don't even know you."

"True, very true."

"So, your best friend realized that you went after his girl...and here you are, looking like that, all alone now."

"Precisely. I don't know if it's this city or what, though, because right now, even with my face all torn up and my body aching all over, I feel relieved. That's not how I'm supposed to feel...is it?"

"I think Ella is right. You are interesting."

I nodded my head in measurable gratitude, and then took another drink.

"What now? This city has a reputation for relentless pursuit of complacency." He asked.

"Yes, but on the flip side, doesn't it also have a relentless pursuit of greatness?"

Julius J. Julius laughed for the first time. "Yep, there's no doubt about it, you're a tourist. No doubt. That's a good one."

I no longer envied his regularity.

"You think you are destined for greatness here in the big city, under all the bright lights?" He added.

"I didn't say I was destined for it. I just pointed out that the opportunity might be there…only if one wishes to take it."

"You're trying to convince yourself to stay because you don't want to face the harsh reality of what transpired between you and your friends. You think staying here will make it all go away. But it won't, it will only make things worse. Trust me, go back to where you came from."

I finished off my drink. "What if I don't want to?"

"Then I'll probably see you more often than not."

This time, he fixed a glass of water for me and told me to drink it.

"What's your name?" He asked.

"Emerson."

"Emerson, where are you from again?"

"Well, right now I live in Denver. I go to school out there."

"What are you studying to do?"

"I don't know. I haven't decided yet."

"You haven't decided. How much longer do you got?"

"Spring will be my final semester."

"Emerson, you've got to get it together. Go back to Denver and figure out what you are going to do with the rest of your life. Believe me, figure it out exactly first, before you do anything, or else you'll end up like me."

"What's wrong with that?"

He laughed for a second time. It must have been a record for such a short span. "I'm from Nebraska, Emerson. I used to have hair on top of my head; I make up for it by having a beard. I use to have a life. I used to have a family. I used to enjoy my job. You don't want to end up like me. Go back to Denver, and just move on and figure out what you want to do. Don't worry about the girl, or your friend. It will either work out or it won't…but you need to go back to find out. You can't avoid your life. And you can't stay here. This city already has too many avoiders."

I felt depressed. Julius J. Julius had said too much. This was one time I wished he would've had his listening ear only on, like most trusty bartenders. I guess you always realize your mistakes after you've made them.

"Unfortunately, I've got very little money left…I didn't think I needed to bring much with me…that's regrettable. I can't just walk right out of town."

"How did you get here?"

"I flew, with my friends."

"Then you fly back with them."

"Julius J. Julius, it's not that easy. I'm not ready for that. Maybe someone like you would be, but I'm a consummate coward. Just one of the many things that was reaffirmed me last night."

"No you're not."

"I appreciate what your trying to do, but it won't work. Like you said earlier, you don't even know me."

Julius J. Julius paused to think for a moment. He looked up at the ceiling as if the answer was up there. Or, maybe he was contemplating if he should do or say what he was about to.

"I'll tell you what Emerson, I like you, and I think you're a good kid. I'm going to make a phone call and see if I can't help get you out of here."

He picked up on my hesitation.

"And yes, you're going to get out of here and go finish up your life in Denver."

"Okay."

Along with feeling depressed, I now felt isolated. I regretted coming here, but I had nowhere else to go.

Julius J. Julius picked up the phone by the cash register and dialed some numbers. He talked too softly for me to overhear. After he hung up, he scribbled something on a waitress' tab-pad. He tore the sheet off from the rest of the tablet and handed it over to me. "Here, follow these directions. This man will help you. Now go on, get out of here."

I didn't even read over the directions before I headed for the door. I was eager to leave. When the air outside hit me, I noticed it was not as crisp or as pleasant as it had been. It was thick and impure. I looked down at the sheet.

Go two blocks south from here and take a left. It's the second door down. Ring the bell if it's not open.

I followed where the instructions directed.

Chapter 19

The door was open. A bell jingled after I pushed on it. I entered into an art gallery. The old lady from yesterday was explaining the meaning of one of the paintings on the wall to an interested customer. I drew their attention after I entered. The old lady greeted me and then directed me up a staircase in the back end of the gallery. The staircase was spiraled and winding. It led to another door. This door was not open. I knocked on it.

After a few minutes the old man, drizzled in paint, entered. "Come on in my boy. I'm sorry to keep you waiting. I hope you understand though…I'm in the middle of a piece. That friend of yours, the singer, inspired me deeply."

The loft was expansive and wide. There was paint and paintings strewn about. There were a few pencil drawings, but not many. A festooning curtain separated the sleeping quarters, which consisted of nothing more than a king-size mattress, from the rest of the area.

"Where do you eat?" I asked.

"I try not to." He replied with a smirk.

I found pleasure in his demeanor. He offered me a scotch drink. I took him up on it.

"Where do you go to the bathroom? Dare I ask?"

The old man smirked again. "You've got a sense of humor. I like that."

He pulled a new three-inch paintbrush out of a bucket that was resting on the paint-stained hardwood floor, and then removed the cellophane from the bristles. He dipped it into yellow paint and splattered it onto one of the canvases. There were three canvases, all of which were clipped to a steel beam running across the ceiling, hanging all the way down to the ground. They were side by side. Each one looked like a separate work in progress, but I knew that the end result would corroborate the three.

"There's a bathroom, with a shower, back in the back over there…just so you don't infer that I'm completely lunatic." He splashed some more paint onto the canvas.

He continued, "Julius J. Julius told me you had a little bit of trouble last night…"

"That's correct…and, before I forget, about last night and the drinks, thank you. Your generosity did not go by unappreciated."

"Don't mention it. It's nice to meet real people from time to time…you don't find that too often here, this town is full of hypocrites…it was the least I could do. That jazz singer, she sure was something. She did a number on me…" More splashing. "I guess her and BoJo are going to ride off into the sunset together, heh?"

"Thanks to you."

He tipped his brush in the air.

"I can hardly believe it."

"Believe it son, believe. That's what it's all about."

The old man was wise even beyond his years. He made me happy. I felt alive being in his presence.

"She was not part of your group, was she? I mean she

wasn't as tight as you and the other two?"

"How could you tell?"

"Besides the obvious..."

"I like your sense of humor too."

We shared a laugh and followed it up with a drink.

"You're different though. The jury's still out on the depth of your authenticity...unlike the singer, man what a woman...but there's optimism within you...hope. There's no denying that. I didn't get that same feeling from the other two...they were together, right?"

"Right."

He set the brush across the top of the yellow paint can. Droplets spattered, intermittently, against the floor after he did so.

"Come over to the window, boy. Just look out there. There's a great big world to discover..."

The old man was inspirational. I took another drink.

"When I was about half your age, my parents, God bless their souls, took me on a trip to this grand resort in Cape Cod. It was the most extraordinary place I had ever visited. Not a care in the world up there. Anyways, my father and mother went into town one day and left me back at the beach...at my request.

I found a concession along the seashore where a man rented out sailboats; little one to two man boats, nothing bigger. I convinced him to let me rent one for the day...told him some story about how my dad was in the navy and how he had taught me how to be an expert sailor. It was complete nonsense, but it worked. I had never sailed before in my life. I was only ten years old for heaven's sake! My father was an engineer from West Virginia, and it was actually only the second time I had ever seen the ocean. First time might as well not count, could have been a lake for all I knew; I was much too young to understand or appreciate it.

So, there I am in this rented sailboat on the great Atlantic Ocean...just me and Old Man Blue and the salty air between us. I had never felt so energetic.

When I got to be about a mile offshore I decided it was probably time for me to turn around. Easier said than done, my boy. Much easier said than done. It was then that I realized the reason my sailing experience to that point had been such a cinch was because I was going with the gales, not against. Needless to say, my feelings of oneness with the sea turned into oneness of fear with my old man's leatherette belt against my backside if I didn't manage to get that boat turned around...and quickly. When the wind carried me out another mile or so, I actually welcomed the prospects of my old man's beating, for at least I would know I was alive!

I could still see the shoreline of the resort from the boat...you can see for miles out on Old Man Blue...but I could also see the shoreline of a fairly sizeable sandbar, which was not recognizable from the resort's shoreline. I figured the sandbar would be my best bet to try and flag down a passing boat for help.

I wafted to the sandbar and waited. No freightliners; no sailboats; no nothing came by the first hour. I waited some more. I must have waited another hour until I saw the first liner come by...have you ever tried to yell across the ocean?"

I shook my head.

"Well let me tell you, you might as well be a mute, cause you can't. The vastness of Old Man Blue soaks all audible sound emitted from any adult human being, much less a scrawny ten year old, right up. After another hour of being stranded on that sandbar, I had had enough. I thought the only way to make it back to the resort was to swim."

"You're kidding?"

"Dead on truth…dead on truth. At first, I tried holding onto the rental boat while swimming, but it was much too heavy to drag that thing through the middle of the Atlantic…and yes, to a ten year old boy it seemed like I was in the middle of the Atlantic. I made it only twenty yards until I let the boat go.

The shore seemed so far away. Each stroke I took seemed to move me further away instead of closer. I remembered I was so frightened I could not stop urinating. Finally, after what seemed like it took an eternity, the shore became within a realistic distance. I don't know how my skinny little bones found the strength, stamina, and energy to pursue, but they did. When I reached the shore I kissed the beach to make sure I was still alive. If I didn't know it then, I knew it after my old man got a hold of me. My ass was sore for a week. He ended up dishing out over twenty dollars for that old rental, and back in those days twenty dollars meant something.

I vowed never to sail again…"

He paused to take a drink. Then he continued, "Nowadays, I've got three sailboats up at our place in the Hamptons and I go sailing every chance I get." The old man smiled and put his arm around me.

"I think I get it."

"Then why are you struggling with a decision? Go after that pretty young woman…even if it is daunting, even if it does involve loss, even if it does mean you have to divulge in a breach of confidence. There is only one concern in these matters. Don't be afraid to accept it. Invite it. Welcome it. Embrace it. Because there's no equal to it. A true friend will understand that and see that. A true friend will not be an obstacle in your hunt for it.

You didn't get all beat up for nothing, now did you? Plus, if it's not true, if it doesn't work out, then you will learn from it and understand yourself better. There's never any harm in trying, and I'm not talking physical harm."

I found myself smiling uncontrollably. The old man had a way about him that made you trust every last word he spoke. I imagined the old lady truly loved him.

"Who knows? Maybe you'll end up drifting away together."

It was after that last statement that I knew what I had to do. The old man saw the realization come into my eyes. He was proud of me. He reached inside his pocket and pulled out a wad of money. Some of the bills had paint splotches on them.

"Here, take this. It should be enough to get you a one-way ticket home."

"I can't take that."

"Then why are you going to? Because you know what's right...now go on."

I took the money from him. "At least give me your address so I can reimburse you after I get back home."

"Money isn't everything, son. You can reimburse me with pride. Trust me, I will be able to feel it if it's right. Now go on."

The old man returned to his canvas and, like that, forgot about my presence altogether. I thanked him in silence and then turned around and walked out the door. I made my way back down the spiral staircase, and as I did so, I felt as if I was descending from the heavens with a newfound sense of purpose, one different than when I first came into this world. It was a sense of rebirth. If I was ever reticent in the past it was because I had no sense of hope. I did not feel like being reserved anymore. Splendid isolation is far from splendid.

The old lady flagged me down before I could exit the gallery. She was still working with the same customer. "I'm just about through here. Please, give me a minute, for I would like to speak to you."

I acknowledged her wishes.

Only thirty more seconds passed until she finished up with the customer. He purchased one of the pieces. I overheard a six-digit number being tossed around before they concluded the deal. The old lady shook the man's hand and said, "We'll pack it properly and then ship it to you in London. Thank you very much."

The customer walked by me with a smile. With his British accent he said, "Isn't this gallery the best one in New York? Buy something. Trust me, it will have a profound impact on your life." He didn't even await a response; he wasn't looking for one. I watched him out the door.

"I trust my old man up there gave you some sound advice?"

"Yes indeed. It was so sound, I've almost forgotten about my aching body altogether. He's given me a different outlook on things. I wouldn't necessarily suggest a new outlook, but one that was previously untapped. He's a good person. Is he your husband?"

The old lady laughed, almost like she was insulted by the question. "He should be so lucky."

"It seems like he's pretty lucky to me. He must be doing something right. He said he had a place up in the Hamptons with sailboats."

The old lady cackled this time, which was followed by a cough. She had heard the story the old man relayed to me before, probably numerous times; and why not, it was a good anecdote.

"Son of a gun loves sailing more than he loves me, and almost more than his art…can you believe that?"

"I guess anything's possible if you believe in yourself." I thought the old lady was testing me. I realized she wasn't when I listened to her response.

"Yes, it's an uplifting story, but don't let its idealism cloud your judgment and common sense. That's what I wanted to talk to you about.

It's obvious you are at war, internally. I knew that yesterday at the bar just for the brief period we were there with you all. I immediately realized much of the cause too, I think.

I want to approach things from a different angle than the old man did...with a story of my own, of course. When I was fourteen I was even more wild than I am now..." She humored herself. "It was during prohibition time and I was sauced up on bathtub gin one night. My friends and I were trying to sneak into this vaudeville theatre when a group of older men, probably in their twenties, came along in their Model A whistling and hollering about...trying to impress us and all. If we weren't so tight from that damn juniper berry mixture, we wouldn't have been...impressed that is...but we were, sad to say. The men told us to hop in their Ford, that they were going to take us to this smoky night club down the way...club, that's funny, they ended up taking us to a park where each one of them had their way with us! There were three of us girl's altogether, and three of them. Perfect for them; they each had a number. Bastards!

My friends and I made a pact that we would never ever speak of the incident, to anyone at anytime...as a matter of fact, you're only one of the few persons I've ever told this too..."

I felt privileged...however, with an underlying suspicion.

"It just so happened I could not keep my incident a secret, for three months later I noticed my belly getting bigger even though my appetite had decreased. I checked myself out with the family doctor, and the bold truth was verified. My parents had to be told.

I didn't know how to break the news to them at first. I was so ashamed. I felt I had done something terribly wrong. I told them only half-truths and they bought off on my story. Then, my father told me he knew of someone who would be willing to take care of it. It! Can you believe that? My father referred to the person inside my belly as It! It was apparently just some object.

The night was dark and rainy and cold. My father accompanied me down the moonlit alley. We came to a door, which was almost falling off of its hinges. A man wearing a white mask over his mouth and nose let us in. I had never been so terrified in my life. The last thing that I remembered was seeing two mucky instruments on top of a shiny steel table…damn, that table was so shiny. I remembered thinking how clean the table looked and how expensive it looked, and the irony of the filthy instruments eerily adorning its top. Damn table.

It wasn't until some years later when I met the old man upstairs and we tried to have a kid that I realized I was permanently damaged."

"That's horrible, just horrible."

The old lady had successfully catapulted all the hope the old man gave me right out of my being. I'm not sure if that was her intent, but if it was, she succeeded.

"Here's the point: even though it is horrible, I'm still here, and I still have the old man. I don't look back on those days and think twice. I don't even regret drinking the illegal gin. It's life! Life is not always going to be roses…in fact, it may seem like there's never any roses along your path at all. But you don't give up looking for them now do you? And, if you find one and if somebody happens to snatch it out of from under you, then so be it. Keep on looking. Keep on journeying down that path in search of another. Life will surprise you when you least expect it. Nobody lives long enough to dwell on the lost roses…on the missed roses. I promise you, there's always going to be another one out there. We wouldn't have a soul if we didn't think that, right? In which case, you would cease to exist. And you exist! I see you right her in front of me…flesh and soul.

Wherever your journey takes you, son, be sensible about it…be realistic about it. Life wouldn't be worth living if we didn't have pain or suffering or loss. You know why? Because of the feeling you get when you experience the reciprocal. Please, just keep that in mind as you go forth."

I believed the old lady complemented the old man's wisdom gracefully and truthfully and absolutely. I couldn't help but to wonder if Ella and I would turn out like that.

Chapter 20

Prior to heading off to the airport, I felt I needed to do something before I left this grand city. I took a cab to the Empire State Building. I went up to the observatory platform and dropped some coins in the viewfinder. I pointed it directly up to the clear blue sky. It was invigorating. No clouds, no smog, no dust, nothing…just azure sky. It wanted desperately to reach out and grab it in hopes of getting lost in it forever. I spent the whole time on that viewfinder looking at the same spot. I wondered what the heavens beyond were thinking of me.

When the time expired, the city no longer seemed unattainable. Actually, it seemed rather dull, almost contented.

It was then that I realized all the worlds had already been conquered.

Part Three
Chapter 21

It was an overwhelmingly desirable feeling, having a sense of purpose, even if it was clouded by confusion and doubt. I had always felt confusion and doubt, that was not foreign to me, but what was unusual was that piercing ability of purpose. For the only time in memory, I was finally aware of what I wanted…what I needed…in order to survive. Ella was my new life-blood. Johnny was nothing to me any longer. He had lost all of his privileges of friendship the very first moment he introduced me to Ella; I was now fully sentient of what his intention was, and the act was unforgivable. I regretted my whole relationship with Johnny, with the gratifying exception of knowing that I opened flesh in his side…penetrated the invincible being that was Johnny Bea…two days ago and caused him temporary pain. I decided to hold onto that thought in hopes of trying to perpetuate that temporary pain status and turn it into one of permanent standing. Johnny had undyingly wounded me. Why should he not suffer the same? Why not…because he's Johnny Bea!

My apartment seemed cleaner than usual. I would never have labeled myself tidy in the past, but then again the past was not what it used to be. And the future was everything that I imagined it to be. I started sifting through my desk drawers in the bedroom I had converted into my study room. The apartment boasted two bedrooms and one full bath. A full kitchen with breakfast room, and a living room completed the unit. It suited me perfectly, not too much space yet not too little…just enough.

I felt my lips form a smile as I encountered an old book I once read when I was younger. The cover had been torn off…or rather eaten off…compliments of a frisky feline named Lyle that used to be part of our family. He was named after my father's favorite football player. The cat's feistiness reminded my father of the feistiness the football player displayed on the field. I just identified the cat as crazy. Thankfully, Lyle had left the rest of the pages intact. Catcher In The Rye. God, I love that book.

I flipped through the pages and landed on a chapter I had highlighted when I was required to read the book in grade school. It was the chapter where Holden is in the washroom with his roommate. Holden is talking with his roommate about an upcoming date with an old girlfriend of his. Girlfriend in the sense of a friend that is a girl, not in the true sense of the word…at least how modern day thinking comprehends it. What a great book! I smiled even wider as I skimmed over the chapter a second time.

I thought of Ella.

I replaced the book back where I found it and then closed the drawer. I opened the one below it up. I didn't ever remember putting anything in that bottom drawer, nor do I ever remember opening it before, but there was something in it. An orange shoebox, as ordinary and as plain as a shoebox could be, was setting inside. My smile still remained, for I figured I was in for a pleasant surprise.

I extended my right hand and placed my fingertips on top of the lid to the box. I shook the box lightly. I discerned there was not a pair of shoes inside it. I removed the lid. Immediately, my smile disappeared. I shut the drawer as rapidly as I could.

I had purchased the ivory-handled, snub-nosed, Thirty-Eight Special my first week of college...the week before I had met Johnny. I bought it from some guy named Morales who lived in the barrio across the street from the east side of campus. He claimed he was giving me a good deal. It cost me fifty dollars, and included the five bullets already loaded in the cylinder. After I had met Johnny I had completely forgot about the weapon. I must have placed it in the bottom desk drawer during my move off campus. Just the sight of that revolver scared me. I never wanted to open that drawer again.

I suddenly felt my throat getting dry. I rushed to the bathroom sink to get a drink of water. When I was finished I heard a pounding on the front door. It startled me, so much so that I had to choke the water down.

I looked in on the desk as I paused on my way to the front door (I hoped it was Ella at the door...I prayed it was Ella at the door...and not Johnny). I must have lost track, standing there staring at that damn desk, because the pounding on the door persisted and increased in intensity. I felt a bead of sweat form above my right eyebrow.

"I know you're in there Em...come on, open up!"

I breathed a little easier. It was Jackie Blasé.

What the hell did she want? I certainly was not in the mood for her right now. All I needed was Ella.

I opened the door with a forced grin.

"Don't look at me that way Emerson Parks..." Jackie barged through the front door with complete disregard for where I was in proportion to it. Thankfully, we were both trim enough that she didn't collide with me. If she would have, I definitely would have been knocked over, that's how hard she came through.

At that moment, I realized the sense of purpose I had believed was now accompanying me had been forged in its nature. It was a false-hope...a pipe dream. Purpose had never found me, and I feared it never would!

Jackie Blasé's demeanor embodied purpose. It oozed from her pores as she stood there fuming at me. She was very intriguing; her eyes were passionate and warm, yet with cold resolution lurking close behind. Never before had she intrigued me so.

"Who the hell do you think you are Emerson Parks? You think that you can just love me and leave me!"

I tried hard not to, but I found myself laughing.

She moved in closer to me and pressed her left index finger against my chest. "Don't you mock me Emerson parks, don't you dare! You might just see me as some floozy, some cheap fling, but let me tell you mister, I'm not! I'm sharp...sharp as a whip. I don't deserve your derision...intentional or unintentional."

I quickly shaped up.

"I allowed all of last week to slide by without notice. I assumed you were thinking things over. I was giving you your space, your time. Men need space and time, so that's what I was doing. But, when the weekend rolled around and I had yet to hear from you, I came a knocking...where the hell have you been? It's now Monday. It has been over a week since we shared the most special act a man and woman can share together. It meant something to me. I deserve an explanation."

She removed her forefinger from my chest and started to cry. I shut the front door with my foot and then embraced her. I felt tremendous sympathy for her. I had trouble remembering why I disliked her so.

She wriggled out of my arms and said, "You can't work your way out of this one Emerson. You're not that charming…no one's that charming."

"I've been in New York."

"New York?"

"Yes. I went on Friday with Johnny and Ella." I didn't feel it necessary to mention Nena McCray.

"Johnny and Ella? What? Why?" I noticed her starting to cool down a little.

"Johnny won the boxing tournament and he decided to take us to New York with the prize money."

Jackie relaxed even more. She shook her head to try and line her thoughts up.

"Well what about the whole week before Emerson? You weren't in New York then. What is it? Do you feel I'm not good enough for you? Do you think you are too good for me?"

Neither one of those questions had ever been posed to me before. I never even considered myself to be one that is capable of eliciting such questions from another, much less a pretty woman who was obviously strongly attracted to me. I felt like a fool. That notion of previous purpose was so distant now, I believe that it had not only left my body altogether, but it was replaced with one of the most unpleasant feelings I had ever experienced.

I stood there silently…pathetically. I did not know how to respond.

Jackie stared at me hard. Then, I saw her heart sink. "Nothing, huh? Then I guess that's my answer. You're an awful person Emerson Parks, just a plain old awful person…nothing more. And that's all you're ever going to be."

I felt tears in my eyes begin to well their lids up.

I grabbed Jackie before she could exit. "Hold on, Jackie. Please! I'm sorry. Let me at least try to explain myself. Please, come to the living room and sit down with me."

Jackie was reluctant to turn around at first, but eventually she did. We walked over to the living room couch. I sat her down initially, and then plopped myself beside her.

She looked at me painfully. She seemed so innocent. I had never seen someone so helpless. I wiped my eyes once and then said, "While I was in New York, and even all of last week before New York, I felt my desires lying with another...Ella to be exact."

"Ella?!"

"Just listen, please, before you go crazy..."

"She's your best friend's girl."

"I know, I know. Please, just listen. I need to get some of this stuff off of my chest anyways..."

"Oh great! Thanks Emerson."

"No, I didn't mean it like that. What you and I shared two weekends ago was irreplaceable. No one can take that from us, not ever. But, my yearnings to be with Ella were, and currently are, too strong to ignore. I can't fight them even if I wanted to. Johnny and I had a falling out this weekend up in New York..."

"I guess so. I was wondering what had happened to your face."

"You should have seen it yesterday, it was much worse. Anyways, the reason we had this falling out, which let me emphasize to you was long overdue, was because of Ella...I think I've fallen for her Jackie."

"You think! You think!"

We sat there in silence for a couple of minutes. I could determine that she was preparing something for me. I didn't know if my face could fit another bruise on it. To my delight, and surprise, she started to speak.

"When I was thirteen, Emerson, I was staying the night over

at a friend's house. It was my best friend's house. My best friend had an older sister, just like I had an older sister. However, my older sister was two years older than my friend's older sister..."

"Okay."

"It was early Sunday morning, six-thirteen to be exact, when my friend's mother came downstairs to where we were sleeping and informed me that I had a phone call. When I picked the phone up the person on the other end was a friend of my mother's. She told me that my sister had been in a car accident, but that everything was all right. She then proceeded to tell me that my uncle would come pick me up and take me home. I didn't think much of it. I mean my mother's friend told me everything was all right. Well, when I went back downstairs to let my best friend know what was going on, it just so happened that her older sister had gone down there while I was talking on the phone. After I told both my friend and her older sister about what was just relayed to me, my friend's older sister said she had heard an extended version of the story earlier that morning. She told me that a friend of hers had called her and told her that one of the passengers in the car, Lucy Loren, was killed in the accident..."

I furrowed my eyebrows as my concern grew. Jackie struggled to keep her composure. I felt like offering a hand of comfort, but didn't.

What was the matter with me?

"Then, my friends older sister told me that my sister was the one driving the vehicle..."

The implications and the possibilities of where the story would go from here were few...but distressing. Jackie was completely in tears now, struggling to find the words. I still did not hug her, or console her in the least. Unquestionably, she was traumatized by this event. I still had no idea how to react.

If I did, I'm sure I wouldn't have. I was too much of a coward. I was too selfish. All I could think of was Ella.

Jackie stood up. "I have never told any part of this story to anyone before, not even the beginning like I have just told you..."

I stood up in front of her. Her tears flowed incessantly, as she had trouble speaking her words fluently. "I have also never told anyone I have loved them before..."

My knees buckled and gave out from under me. I found myself back on the couch. That was more powerful of a blow than Johnny could have ever dealt me.

As Jackie opened the door she said, "Maybe one day you'll desire to hear the rest of the story."

She cried all the way down the hall. I cried too.

Chapter 22

I waited at the corner bus stop for the downtown courier to arrive. Before I decided to take the bus to Ella's place I stopped off at the local liquor store and picked up a fifth of Jack Daniels and a pack of cigarettes. Neither vice tasted as good as they had before the trip to New York. I was beginning to despise that town.

Across the street from the bus stop there was a playground full of young children enjoying the fresh air while frolicking amongst the various amenities the playground boasted. One boy, in particular, caught my eye. He was standing off in the corner close to the fence that barricaded the playground and the children within it. He was twirling an oak leaf. He had his back turned to the rest of the kids. The expression on the boy's face made me feel even worse than I already was feeling.

I took a drag off of my cigarette. I surveyed the other kids for a few moments. Not a one even attempted to make the boy in the corner feel part of the crowd. There was one little girl who looked over in his direction, but her concern lied with a pink car that passed by, not the isolated boy. I had trouble grasping the indecency...or inhumanity.

I walked across the street. When I approached the boy I said, "Hey little man, what are you doing there?" The boy didn't even look up at me. The chain-linked fence separated us. I knelt down to be on his level, instead of above.

"What does it look like I'm doing?" The young boy's voice was very high and extremely frigid.

"I'm sorry, that was a pretty foolish question. Of course, you're twirling an oak leaf."

He finally looked over at me. He had the most radiant blue eyes I had ever seen. Unfortunately, they were not noticeable to the unenlightened for they were marked and masked by insecurity.

"How come you're not over there with the rest of the kids playing?"

The boy twirled the leaf faster in his hands and shrugged his shoulders.

"Don't they like you?"

He shrugged his shoulders again.

"Don't you like them?"

This time, there was no response at all.

"You know, when I was your age I didn't have many friends either…as a matter of fact now that I come to think of it, I didn't have any friends."

The boy's interest was momentarily aroused. "Did you get picked on?"

"No. Not that I can remember. I think I was just different. I wasn't interested in the same things the other kids were…I guess." I answered.

"What were you interested in?" The boy was mature beyond his years. I thought of the old couple in New York.

I extinguished my cigarette on the concrete. "I don't know."

At that moment, I was beginning to think that it might have been a bad idea coming over to this playground to try and cheer this boy up. So far, it was apparent that I was not succeeding in that effort, and in truth I was becoming more depressed.

I refocused the conversation back on him. "What about you? What types of things interest you?"

He twirled the oak leaf faster. "This interests me…a lot."

"That's good. That's real good. Everybody needs something to be interested in."

I noticed the word interest kept surfacing. It reminded me of how Ella thought I was interesting.

The boy stopped twirling the leaf. He recognized the whiskey bottle protruding out of the inside pocket of my jacket. "Is that what you're interested in?"

Firstly, I looked at him unemotionally. Then, I shook my head and averted my eyes in embarrassment.

"How come you are carrying it around in your pocket then?"

"I don't know?" Boy was I pitiable.

"That's exactly what my daddy always says: I don't know. He says I don't know to everything…that is, when he is able to speak. I think that is the worst phrase in the English language: I don't know. I'd much rather just keep silent and shrug my shoulders if I really didn't know something, which in many cases I don't. But, I'm only ten years old. I'm not supposed to know stuff. But you, you're probably twice my age, and my daddy is three times my age, you guys are supposed to know stuff."

I kept silent and shrugged my shoulders. The boy smiled, but it was a smile of disappointment, sadness, and regret. I believe he regretted living in such a world: a world where people either don't know stuff or claim that they don't know stuff. Whichever way it's perceived, it's not good. And this boy made me realize that. I felt the same way he did.

"I suppose the stuff I do know is useless. It's just a bunch of information floating around in this mixed up head of mine.

There's nothing there to connect all of it together...to make it fluid so I can apply it to something."

"Maybe it's not useless. Maybe you just haven't found that something to apply your knowledge to."

Knowledge, I didn't have any knowledge.

"I wouldn't have coined you for an optimist." I said.

"What's that?" He asked.

"Forget it."

"You see, that right there. Older people always think younger people are too young to understand stuff. Maybe that's why everybody goes around saying I don't know."

I smiled at the boy. "Alright. Being an optimist means that you have a positive, or good, outlook on life situations and future situations...always seeing the possibility of good in things, instead of always seeing the bad things that might happen."

"I'm no optimist then."

"Oh, okay. Your last statement made it sound like you were."

"That's because I'm young. I don't know what I'm talking about."

My smile evolved into a laugh.

"How come you're not at work? Or school? Or are you a deadbeat? I know a lot of deadbeats. It wouldn't surprise me if you were one, even if you don't really look like one. Are you a deadbeat?"

"Of course I'm not. I go to school at the university down the street."

"Why aren't you there right now?"

"I've got some important stuff happening in my life right now. Stuff that I'm trying to figure out."

"I thought you told me you didn't have anything to apply all that useless information in your head to."

"I did. Information is different than emotion. You can't ignore emotion, even if you don't like it. Information you can."

"Why not?"

I shrugged my shoulders.

"The teachers here tell me that when I start feeling bad, or confused, or angry, then all I need to do is think of a happy place and imagine myself in it. It never works for me, though. I have trouble imagining a happy place."

"Why don't you imagine doing what you're doing right now?"

"Twirling this oak leaf interests me, I didn't say it made me happy. It doesn't."

"Is there any part of this school that you like?"

He shrugged his shoulders.

This boy was even more incredible than the old couple from New York. "Is there any part of your life that you do like?"

He shrugged again. "Is there any part of your life that you like?"

His question threw me off guard, so much so that I almost lost my balance. He looked hard at me, with those luminous blue eyes. I realized that it wasn't his insecurity that surrounded those eyes...it was a reflection of mine.

I pulled out my whiskey bottle and took a drink. When I replaced it back in my inside pocket the boy said, "It's okay if you don't have anything right now that you like..."

I cut the boy off before he could finish. "Wait a second. I do. That's why I'm waiting at the bus stop over there. Ella. I like Ella. I love Ella. That's what I like in my life."

"Is Ella your girlfriend?"

"Not exactly."

The boy laughed. "I find myself thinking that a lot...not exactly. That's almost as bad as I don't know."

Just then, the bell rang. "I've got to go back in now." And

with that, he ran off inside the schoolhouse.

I remained kneeling on the ground and lit another cigarette. I took another drink of whiskey. I had never felt so miserable in my life.

When I rose, I was mystified to find that, now, not only thoughts of Ella raced through my head, but thoughts of Jackie as well. I took another drink and walked back over to the bus stop. Immense pain found my head as I struggled to divert my attention away from my thoughts.

When the bus arrived, the pain left. I dropped my coin into the money receptacle and assessed the seating situation. There were not very many passengers on the bus. I opted for a seat towards the back of the bus. There was no other passenger within three seats of me.

I thought of my parents and why they never had any more children, other than me. I thought of my education, and what it meant to me. I thought of my previous relationships with women, and how inadequate they were. I thought of my previous relationships with men, and how few there were. I thought of Johnny. I thought of Ella. I thought of New York. I thought of Jackie. But, most importantly, and most despondently, I thought of myself, and my life.

I had never felt so alone. Even while in search of what I felt might be my only chance at love, I still was completely aware that I was wholly singular and solitary. As much as I tried, I failed in escaping these thoughts. The boy at the playground sent me into this mental tailspin. I did not blame him though. If anything, I should've probably thanked him...but I was too selfish for that. I hoped he didn't turn out a coward like me. I knew he wouldn't. He was a good kid, a real good kid. I wished I were like him when I was that age. I wished I were like him right now.

I got to thinking about our conversation again. I analyzed

some of my answers. I wondered if that was the little boy's intention all along. I kept going back to the I don't know comments. He was right on about the repulsion of the phrase. I tried to remember back to when I first used that phrase. Surprisingly, the memory found its way into the forefront of my consciousness.

I was thirteen years old. I was very impressionable, just like most thirteen year olds. But, for some reason, I believe I was exceedingly impressionable. I was in my mathematics course and the whole class was involved with a game that had to do with solving word problems on the blackboard. I never liked mathematics.

The way the game went was like this: there were two teams, a green team and a yellow team. The teacher had assigned each student to one of the two teams. I was assigned to the yellow team. Each round the two teams would face-off against one another. The player from the team who could answer the problem the fastest, and who could answer it correctly, would decide the winner of the round. I was matched up against Missy Margoline. She was a real mathematics whiz. I was extremely nervous because Missy and I were the last pairing to go and the two teams were all tied up. The winner of our round would determine the winner of the game. All of my teammates cheered me on anxiously. The same went for Missy.

I didn't even press my chalk against the board. Everyone on my team, the yellow team, was so disappointed. The green team was very excited they won, but I believe they were more stunned that I didn't even attempt the problem. When I turned around and faced the crowd, I felt numb and empty. I didn't feel embarrassed, like most normal teenagers would have; I just felt numb and empty. It was awful. When the proctor asked me what I was doing, I answered 'I don't know, I guess I'm just a coward,' and then I walked out of the classroom. Nothing was the same, internally, from that moment on.

When I got off of the bus, I didn't feel as eager to see Ella. I took another drink off my bottle and headed for The Montebello. I saw both Johnny's and Ella's cars in the parking lot as I entered through the security gate. I didn't feel much like encountering Johnny; I knew that for sure. He probably wanted to kill me.

Numbness and emptiness enveloped my being as I knocked on Ella's door.

Chapter 23

I pressed my ear against the door to see if I could hear anything going on inside. I could not. I knocked softly.

"Who is it?" Ella asked. Her voice was coarse, not as assured as normal. I presumed she was still feeling the effects of the right Johnny landed on her face.

I knocked softly again to verify I was still there. I didn't want to speak from outside of the door, in fear of Johnny being inside and recognizing my voice. I knew Johnny most likely was inside, and I didn't want to chance it.

Ella cracked the door.

"What are you doing here?" She whispered too loudly. Apparently, my mere presence upset her. She looked back inside the apartment hastily and then turned back to me. "Johnny's here. If he knows it's you, I don't know what the hell he'll do…hasn't your face been damaged enough?"

"Hasn't yours? How can you still be with him after what he did?"

"Why were you best friends with him for three years? I love him Emerson."

"What are you saying? Just two days ago you and I

shared..."

"Hush! Keep it down." Ella interrupted. She was very angry, and had trouble herself keeping the noise down. She looked back inside again.

"Who is it Ella?" Johnny shouted from inside.

"Nobody. Its just some solicitor." She answered. She was not convincing.

"We need to talk. Now, we can do it the hard way or..." "Meet me at The Hill in two hours. We will talk then. Now go!"

I heard Johnny stomping through the apartment, making his way towards the door, as Ella shoved me back. I gazed hard into Ella's eyes to try and decipher what was going on behind them. I could read nothing.

"Is that Emerson? Son-of-a-bitch! Doesn't he learn? God damn it! I'm going to finish this once and for all."

I caught Johnny out of my peripheral. He was rounding the hallway's corner. "The Hill in two hours, Ella. You better be there!" I finished. Then, I took off running.

I don't believe Ella allowed Johnny to make it out the door to either chase me or to scream at me, because I did not hear any footsteps or words following after my trail.

When I made it back street side, the weather had drastically turned from bright sun to cold hard rain. The blatant coincidence between the weather and my inner-strife was drawn. However, I felt it was just too obvious to be reflective of the truth. I looked up towards the heavens and allowed the cold drops to splatter freely against my face. It felt terrific; not cleansing terrific, but reality terrific...as if I was so naïve to the truth that the heavens had to help me out by slapping me in the face. Wake Up! They were telling me. I was not so naïve.

I walked around downtown Denver for a while as I finished off my bottle of Jack Daniels. Once the bottle was emptied, I jumped back on the bus and headed for campus. I was feeling pretty wound up, which was what I desired. The upcoming encounter with Ella would be very testing, I knew that, and the liquor and its effects only enhanced my mental state, not detract it. The boy at the schoolyard would have disagreed, and disapproved, but he was just a boy. The old couple from New York would have understood my reasoning; hell, they would have encouraged the releasing powers of alcohol.

In Vino Veritas. That was something I learned in high school. I never laid any credence to it until I actually got drunk for the first time and told my parents they were 'Industrialists to the core, not transcendentalists, and that any attempt to believe otherwise would be feign and futile.' I was seventeen, and my parents and I were at my cousin's wedding in Naples, Florida. The ceremony was on the beach, overlooking the Gulf of Mexico. If there was ever a time to get drunk and watch the sunset, that was it. I wasn't prepared, however, for the discarding of inhibitions that went along with taking that first swill of cool Russian vodka. The vodka was compliments of my washed out uncle. He told me he wished I was his son that night, and how he wished I were the one getting married to the bride. He said she was too good for somebody like his real son, and that he would just ruin it...he would just screw things up in no time at all and then come crawling back to him. My uncle gave the marriage six months. He was two months shy of the reality. I thought my uncle was the greatest man alive that night. No one had ever expressed any sentiments like that to me before; no one had even expressed anything remotely close.

It wasn't until the next day that it was apparent my uncle's priming and primping...along with his continual offer, and subsequent supply, of liquor...was what instigated my newfound penchant for crass and brutal honesty. I regretted telling my parents what I had told them. I took something away from them that night.

My uncle didn't even remember telling me what he had told me, but I still believe what he said. In Vino Veritas.

I needed a cigarette when I stepped off of the bus. I decided to walk around campus before I headed over to The Hill. It was still raining. There was hardly anybody roaming around campus like I was. In fact, there was no one. I was reminded of an old movie I saw one time as a child. There was this hard-looking man wearing this dusty old leather jacket walking through the streets of this seemingly desolate ghost town. He ambled up to this saloon and entered. When he entered, he came upon a ripened and frail old man sitting at one of the card tables. The old man told him that there were only two ways to get out of the town alive, for some unknown force haunted it. He explained that this unknown force had already killed every last one of the townspeople, except for him. The man in the dusty leather jacket asked him why he had not fallen victim to this mysterious force. The old man responded by saying 'Because I chose the worse of two options.' The man in the dusty leather asked what the two options were. The old man held out both his hands; each hand was clasped shut, as if holding onto something. The old man instructed the man in the dusty leather jacket that he did not have to choose either option, but if he didn't then he would fall victim to the unknown force. The man in the dusty leather looked at the old man with cautious suspicion. He studied him very closely…very closely. Then he said, 'I'll take my chances,' and turned and drifted right out of town. When he got to the edge of the town, a heavy rain hit and washed all of the dust off of his leather jacket. What a great movie. That's what I was reminded of as I walked through this desolate college campus.

How come my greatest memories are all associated with fiction, or escaping from reality? Rachmaninoff; The Catcher

In The Rye; the drunken night with my uncle when I basically told my parents they were a sham; and the movie. I loved those memories. As of this moment in time, they seem to be the only memories that I love. Boy, is that sad? Why can't I love normal memories? Why can't I love memories about going fishing in the summertime with my father? Why can't I love memories about listening to my mother recite poetry on the front porch of our house, written by her own hand? Why can't I love memories about losing my virginity? Why can't those be the memories that I love? Those are real.

I was bereft of life. I was not real. The old man in New York was mistaken. Authenticity was nowhere to be found in these blasted bones of mine.

Perhaps, I was just too befuddled.

I walked around campus some more and found myself in front of one of the classrooms looking in. It was despairing, demoralizing, and disparaging when I did not recognize one familiar face…not one single person did I know. I walked over to another set of classroom windows and looked inside. Same result; I did not recognize anyone in there either. How could this be? I was in my final year here. I started to panic as I went to a third classroom. It did not give me a sense of relief when the only face I recognized was the one of the underclassman who tried to thwart Johnny of his pride during Chuck Wylie's Saturday evening pub-crawl at the first of the year, just three weeks ago. The sight of him actually increased my paranoia, for I feared I held numerous similarities to him. I stared at him. I didn't want to stare at him, but something beyond my control compelled me to keep looking at him.

When the whole classroom…a classroom full of strangers with dull expressions on their faces…turned in my direction, I finally snapped out of it. The underclassman that I was staring at looked at me very nervously. I pulled my coat over my head, concealing everything but my eyes. I think I was embarrassed for him, not me. There was something within him that caused me disconcert. But, the strange thing was, I felt pity for me, not for him, even though I was feeling embarrassed for him. He buried his head in his palms as I turned and walked away. I still had my coat draped over my head.

I headed for The Hill with saturated eyes. On my way to The Hill, I found myself thinking about my parents again. What was going on? I guess it was the previous memory of my cousin's wedding. I don't know. I rarely thought about my parents. Actually, the only time I thought of them was when I thought about what they wanted to be instead of who they really were. Maybe I had been giving them too hard of a time...a bad wrap about it...within my own mind that was. I have never once voiced my opinions to them, while sober of course. My parents weren't bad people. They weren't bad people at all. They were good people.

My father tries as best as he can to be a good Dad and a good Husband. Sometimes, especially before now, I felt he had done a better job at being a husband than a father. I believed he was quite lax in the fathering department, actually...at least that's how I used to feel.

When I was in the fifth grade I tried out for soccer. I was trying to please my father. I made the team. Everybody made the team at that age. I was abysmal at the sport...just terrible. Most of the time I found myself standing away from the action (perhaps engaging in a light jog to make it look like I was at least exuding some effort towards my interest in the game, but that was only when I thought the coach was watching) trying to avoid the ball altogether. The few times that the ball did come my way I would swing my left leg at it as quickly as I could so as to get it away from me. I wasn't even left-footed for crying out loud! I was really dreadful. But, each and every single game my father would show up, no matter if it was raining or snowing or what. Every game he always attended. He didn't always drive me to the game; the coach had a carpool, which I dismayed but felt obligated to join in on from time to time. Why do kids always feel obligated to do stuff that is assigned to them? What are they afraid is going to happen if they don't? Maybe the better question is why do parents feel their kids are obligated to do that type of stuff. It's all pretty much nonsense. Anyways, every game my father attended. He had to know I was horrible at the sport. Everybody knew. Even the other parents knew. I wondered if he had to defend me in front of the other parents. He would have too...and he would have done it proudly. I see that now, whereas I didn't use to. My father was a good man, as much as I hate to admit that to myself. I hate to admit it because it's true, and if it's true then that means I've been living the better part of my years in illusion. I didn't want to be illusional anymore. My father was so good, so encouraging, that he even bought me a professional style soccer ball along with a high-dollar pair of soccer cleats that year for my birthday. I never used either gift though. I just stuffed them away in my closet, along with numerous other things. My father knew this, but it didn't bother him. He had to have seen how awful I was.

My mother worked at the local library in our hometown. She loved books. Her favorite book, which was surprising to me, was Hemingway's The Sun Also Rises. She made me read it once. I think it was that same year my dad bought me the ball and cleats. The book didn't do much for me though. My mother has been to both Paris and Pamplona; she's even seen the running of the bulls and her fair share of bullfights. She understands the piece I guess. I still do not. Her father was also in his prime during The Jazz Age...maybe that has something to do with it. He probably told her a lot of neat anecdotes and interesting stories. Besides her making me read The Sun Also Rises I can remember she used to make me peanut butter and jelly sandwiches everyday for lunch when I was really young, and when I still only went half-day to school. She used to join me in the living room. I always believed she was eating peanut butter and jelly sandwiches just like me, but now I realize she wasn't. It was just wishful thinking on my part. I guess I should have just been pleased that she joined me for lunch. Not many other kids could have said that their mothers joined them for lunch. I remember we always watched the same television program while we ate our lunch: old reruns of Leave It To Beaver. I loved that show at the time. I despise it now. Besides working in the library, my mother also volunteered at a thrift shop on an avenue ten miles east of our house in an unruly part of town. She worked the cash register and helped to tag and fold the used clothing. My father didn't much like her working there. She certainly didn't need to. She didn't even need to work at the library. She wanted to though, and that was all that mattered when you got down to it. My mother had a good heart.

One time, the two of them took me to a movie downtown. It was a Sunday matinee. It was the hottest movie at the time. They had heard everybody raving about it: their friends, the newspapers, and all the talk radio shows. I don't know how, but they didn't realize it was too violent and too profane for such a young boy. It was not a movie for someone my age, at the time, to see. It was a movie about a cab driver. I can't remember the name, but I know it had some famous actors in it. My parents were terribly apologetic afterwards, but even though they expressed their sorrow for taking me, I still never understood why they didn't take me out of that theatre after they realized the movie was unsuitable for someone like me. I was humiliated. I tried to close my eyes through the whole picture. That movie was so long. My parents were terribly apologetic afterwards. It's amazing how vulnerable one's parents can seem when they are terribly apologetic. I have never seen that movie since, nor do I desire to.

Another time, while at a company picnic…my father is a developer and certain contractors would always invite him to their company picnics…I was eating a hot dog at a rusty colored picnic bench with my parents. It was just the three of us at this picnic bench. I asked my parents why I didn't have any brothers or sisters. They both were shocked into silence. They couldn't, and didn't, move for what seemed like an eternity. Then, my mother looked over at my father, just with her eyes, and raised her eyebrows. My father breathed heavily and hung his head. Then, he went into some long spiel that I couldn't even comprehend. I didn't understand either one of their reactions at the time, and I certainly didn't understand my father's long-winded explanation. I understand now.

My parents were good people.

I needed a drink. I was relieved to be at the entrance to The Hill. The rain had stopped.

Ella was sitting at one of the booths with a strange, yet deliberate, look on her face. She had two empty glasses in front of her and one full one. Before I joined her, I walked over to Jane and ordered a shot of whiskey. After I took it, I ordered vodka on the rocks like I always did when I was at this joint.

I felt hesitation of the heart transform into weakness of the legs as I approached the booth. Ella didn't look at me until I sat down across from her.

"Before you say anything, or go off on a rant, let me speak. I've never known anyone quite like you Emerson. As I have told you before, you are a very interesting person…"

What was it that attracted me to her? I was beginning to forget. Her face looked as pitiable as her words sounded. "I don't want to hear this, Ella. I know where you're going…I'm very confused too. All your talk about Drifting and finding a mate to Drift with affected me something fierce. I think I am in love with you, but as of right now I just don't know…maybe I'm in love with your ideas."

She took a drink, clumsily, and then said, "You don't love me Emerson. You don't even know me."

"People always say that when they are scared. How can an intelligent woman like your self be more scared of me than someone like that bastard, Johnny? Who, in case you forgot, gave you that enormous welt on your face just days ago; the same guy who all but deformed mine, his former best friend."

"At least your marks seem to be improving. Mine has gotten worse."

"Please, don't try and evade the question."

"I'm not trying to evade the question, Emerson." She was starting to get a little fumed…a little huffy. Good. This is what I needed.

She finished off her drink and ordered another one. She waited until Jane brought the drink over to our table until she continued. I lit a cigarette and waited. "Johnny is a good man, a strong man…internally Emerson. He makes me feel secure."

I couldn't believe it. She had to be trying to convince herself. She couldn't even look at me as she spoke those words.

"Makes you feel secure? Ella, I do believe you pulled the wool over my eyes. I was way off about you. Your good, I'll give you that. Unfortunately, and inexplicably, I still feel something in the depths of my soul for you…I am really having trouble understanding it momentarily though."

"What's that supposed to mean?"

"It means that if Johnny Bea makes you feel your secure, then you are just as delusional as I was." She looked at me for the first time. "That's right Ella, for three years of my life I befriended Johnny, and, as of today, in fact as of the day I met you, I believe I finally realized why. So yes, Ella, I was delusional for more than a thousand straight days…but not anymore. Not to mention, my situation was much different than yours. Friends are different than lovers…far different. You can't be so naïve as to not know that?"

"I'm not naïve Emerson."

"You sure are sounding and acting like you are."

"You haven't even given me a chance to finish what I was going to say. You don't even know what I am planning to do here!"

"It was pretty damn obvious when I woke up all battered and bruised in that shoddy hotel room back in New York and found that you weren't there as to what your decision, or position, or whatever, was. And, it was reconfirmed today when I came knocking on your door and…lo and behold…Johnny's back in your bedroom; no doubt apologizing for his behavior in the best way he knows how."

"You're out of line, Emerson."

"I'm out of line! Forgive me, Ella, but I do remember sharing something pretty special with you back before we got all beat up. That wasn't just some roll in the hay for me. If anyone is out of line, it's you!" For some reason, my thoughts instantly focused on one person, and one person only: Jackie Blasé…only for a moment, and then the moment was gone.

"If you don't calm down I'm going to leave."

Never before do I remember myself voicing my rage, and with at least a shred of confidence. The liquor must have been getting to me. I ordered another drink from Jane.

"Was it meaningless to you?" I was so undone that I inadvertently asked a question I had no desire of wishing to hear the answer to. Actually, I felt I already knew the answer. I just didn't want to hear the response trickle from Ella's lips.

It was too late. Ella looked me straight in the eye with one of those deadly stares. "How dare you ask me that?"

She slammed her drink down her throat and ordered Jane to bring her another one along with the one she was bringing me. Needless to say, Ella had not responded the way I thought she was going to. I should have been contented, and even pleased, with her response…hell, I should have been ecstatic…but to my bewilderment, I was not. I hated to admit that I felt numbness and emptiness.

I wished Jane would hurry up with the damn drinks. I fell back in the booth and watched Ella closely. "I'm sorry," was all I could think of to say.

Where the hell were those damn drinks? It seemed like Jane was intentionally taking her measly time to get them to us…more importantly, to get mine to me.

When Jane finally arrived at the table, I snatched my drink out of her hand before she could offer it to me and swallowed the whole thing down like I was some ritualistic drunk. Then, I ordered another one while she still stood over the table. She looked at me cruelly with one eye. She seemed to be upset with me, or disappointed. She turned and walked away floutingly. What the hell had I done to her?

"You should be sorry, Emerson, getting all emotional and hacked off when you haven't even heard me out."

I retreated with my eyes, and then leaned back up against the table.

She continued, "You and I did share something special back in New York, and no one will ever be able to strip that away from me…not Johnny, not you, not anyone. I will always hold onto that memory firmly…" She collapsed her hands over her heart. It was too melodramatic for me. I thought she was being insincere. "But I feel that New York is where it belongs. We don't need to…we can't…bring it back here. I don't want to bring it back here. It was special, Emerson...yes, there's no denying that...but it was temporary."

I almost preferred that she just told me that the time we spent, and the intimacy we shared, meant nothing to her...that it was a lapse in judgment, or a haphazard attempt at vengeance or justice. That's the response I anticipated.

Now, with these words she just anted up, I became even more distraught. Positively, I wouldn't have been flustered if it meant nothing to her... oh no, not at all. It might have even made me feel less numb and less empty if she had just murmured the response I was looking for. But, she didn't.

"I've got to see, I've got to know, if Johnny and I have a future. I owe him that..."

I laughed out loud, unwillingly.

"Emerson!"

I held my hand up in disingenuous condolence. This whole situation was turning into a mockery. Hell, I believe it was a charade from the beginning. This was disgusting.

Jane returned with my drink. I sucked half of it down, but didn't finish it off. My cigarette burnt out. I needed another one.

"Everybody is allowed a mistake or two, Emerson."

I shook my head in pure disbelief. "I can't believe I ever even thought of you as a feminist."

"I never said I was a feminist, Emerson."

"No, I know. I just can't believe I considered you one at first. You said you were an existentialist...I remember."

"Yes. I believe in freedom of choice and the responsibility and subsequent consequences, if any, that go along with that free choice. I made a choice, and I suffered the consequences..." She displayed the welt on her face. "Now, I am moving on, trying to make things better in this indifferent universe...trying to make myself better."

"And you believe Johnny is going to help you in that effort?"

"I don't know, but I am willing to find out…more than willing, actually."

She took a long drink and then asked me something I wasn't expecting. "Emerson, besides me, have you ever been in love?"

My entire disposition shifted into one of awkwardness. What was she trying to do? "Of course I have been in love."

"With who?"

"Many a girls."

"Name one."

"Well, there's you, and…" My head started to hurt, and I fell silent.

"And who?"

At once, I could feel the transformation from awkwardness to fury literally taking place within my body. Instead of just my head hurting, now my whole body did.

Ella picked up on this. "Okay Emerson, it's okay. Many people never find love."

I slammed my fist against the table. Ella jumped in surprise. She was more amazed than scared by my reaction. She thought I was a coward too.

"Calm down, Emerson. It's okay."

"It's not okay, Ella. I suppose now you are going to tell me that all that stuff about Drifting was just small talk…just a bunch of fodder you fed me, the big fat interesting cow! Why the hell would you tell me all of that stuff if you didn't believe in it? Do you think so low of me that it humored you to placate me like that?"

"No Emerson, not at all, just the opposite. I swear to you, I wouldn't lie to you. I think more of you and your potential than I think of myself. You are much more than interesting Emerson. I'm the one who's envious. That's why I told you about Drifting and the Drifter's code of ethics…"

"Oh yes, of course. And tell me, Ella, just what exactly is the Drifter's code of ethics?"

"You already know the answer."

"I don't believe that. I don't believe you!"

I felt like getting up and leaving, but I couldn't get my legs to stir for the life of me. I think I understood why my legs were not cooperating with the instructions my mind was giving them, however.

"You've got to believe me, Emerson, I wouldn't lie to you."

"Do you honestly believe in all that stuff? Tell the truth."

"Of course I do. I wouldn't lie to you."

"Do you think Johnny is your Drifting mate then?"

"Like I've told you before, I don't know, but it's worth it to try and find out."

"What about me, Ella? Why do you think it would not be worth it to try and find out with me?"

The most eerie, deafening silence fell over our table at that moment. I wanted to leave so badly, but I just could not move.

Ella looked down at the ground and said, "I don't know."

I wish she would have just shrugged her shoulders and kept silent.

Chapter 24

Ella continued on for a while, but the words she spoke were the same ones as before only structured differently. It was mind numbing to listen to her, so I didn't. I faded into thoughts of Johnny. I must have really been wound up, because the last thing I wanted to do was think about Johnny. I couldn't help it though. Even my subconscious couldn't think of any alternative thoughts. Johnny's Brawn was quite substantial, and impressive at that...that had been established...but I believe his ability to manipulate was what had encapsulated me; manipulation, of course, is a negative characteristic. I didn't think it at the time. The realization only comes after the fact. Johnny manipulated the hell out of me. I was like dough in his hands. He could mold me into his liking. Why?

I would do anything for him. If he would ask me to write a speech for him, I would do it. If he would ask me to go pick up some food for him in the middle of the night because he was too tired, I would do it. If he would ask me to lie for him, I would do it. I would do anything for him.

This one time, two years ago, Johnny and I went up to the mountains to go snow skiing, just the two of us. Neither one of us had a girlfriend at the time…come to think of it, neither one of us ever had a girlfriend throughout the whole time we knew one another, until recently when Ella entered the picture. We got together with girls, of course, but neither one of us ever held one of those girls in high enough esteem to put forth the effort to pursue a relationship, much less an exclusive one. Johnny always got more girls than I did. It was something I never understood, and still don't; I am much more attractive and handsome than he. I suppose Johnny just has a way about him…knows the right buttons to push at the right times. Anyways, we were staying in a sleepy town named Frisco, which was about twenty minutes away from Breckenridge. All of the accommodations in the Breckenridge area were filled to capacity, so we ended up in Frisco.

The first night we were there, we went to this bar directly across the street from where we were staying called The Moose's Mouth. We were underage at the time, but each one of us had false identification stating that we were of legal drinking age. Upon entering The Moose's Mouth, we were immediately greeted by a bouncer. Johnny gave him a look like he owned the place, therefore the bouncer only asked me for my identification. Johnny had already made his way up to the bar while I was still at the door presenting my artificial license to the scrutinizing bouncer. The bouncer studied that damn license forever. He would rub his fingers over the face of it a couple of times and then look back up at me; he must have repeated that process four or five times. I looked over at Johnny for some help, a few times during this examination, but he was already preoccupied with the atmosphere of The Moose's Mouth. It was as if I wasn't even with him. Maybe, that's how he wanted the others around the bar to perceive it; that I was just some underage schoolboy and he was Big, Bad Johnny Bea: the ultimate at everything that means anything! At about the same time Johnny got his first beer, I was denied admittance. I just turned around and walked out with my head down.

As I walked through the snow-covered streets of the diminutive town, I noticed an old, wooden wagon wheel resting upon the side of a red brick building down this one particular alley. It interested me deeply. I felt like striding over to the wheel and touching it. It reminded me of the pioneers. I always thought about being a pioneer when I was younger. Until recent years, I actually thought I was capable of becoming one. But that thought passed, right along with many of my other thoughts; just another one of those things inside my head floating around looking for some sort of direction, or at the very least, instruction…useless stuff.

I walked over to the wagon wheel. Before I could stretch my arm out to reach it, however, a boy a few years younger than myself at the time jumped out from behind it and scared me half to death. I fell hard, heels over head right into the snow, that's how bad he surprised me. The boy laughed and laughed at first, but then he offered me his hand.

After he helped me up he said, "I'm sorry about that, I just couldn't resist the temptation. I saw you coming from the street there, all intent on this old wagon wheel here, and I just couldn't help myself. I'm sorry. My name is Mikey, but my friends at school call me The Frisco Kid."

I laughed, and then gathered myself together. "Are you Joking?"

"Hell no, I ain't joking!" He exclaimed, rather vehemently too.

He knew I was older than him. He told me he was sixteen, but I knew his age was closer to fourteen. Since Johnny was back at The Moose's Mouth, and since I was feeling somewhat abandoned and isolated, I asked The Frisco Kid if he wanted to join me in a couple of beers back at the motel room. Johnny and I had made a run to the store first thing when we got into Frisco and stocked up on beer and liquor.

The Frisco Kid walked back to the motel room with me, and the two of us started drinking some beers together. I thought I was going to regret inviting him at first, but after we got to talking, I didn't. He was really quite engaging, actually. He told me this story about how him and his father were out taking a hike through the mountains one summer afternoon when they came upon this black bear. He said that the black bear was very hostile and that his father demanded that Mikey run while he retained the bear's attention. The Frisco Kid did as his father wanted, but he only ran about fifty yards off into the woods. He understood that even though his father was extremely brave and strong that he was still no match for the black bear. The Frisco Kid heard the bear roaring and howling off in the distance, while he was safe in the woods, but he did not hear any screams from his father; this disheartened him much, and he felt that his father might have perished. After about a half an hour or so, The Frisco Kid could no longer hear the bear's roars and howls so he thought it was safe to head back and recover his father. When he came upon his father he was extremely delighted, for his father did not perish. He was unconscious and battered, but not dead. The Frisco Kid's father was lying on the ground with his clothes all shredded, and his face all bloodied, but he did not have any chunks of flesh bitten out of him or claw marks anywhere noticeable; The Frisco Kid was elated after he recognized this. His father was not too badly hurt considering the circumstances. But, he knew he still needed help though. However, when The Frisco Kid turned around to run back and seek assistance, he found that the bear had set a trap; the bear had been waiting for the young boy to come back and rescue his father. The Frisco Kid's first instinct was to run. He took off as fast as his little legs could move. The black bear chased after him, while leaving the boy's father still lying there unconscious. The boy was fast, but not as fast as the bear, so when he felt the animal gaining on him he found a tree and climbed it quickly. This was something The Frisco Kid had heard never to do when being chased by a bear, but he had no other option he thought. He had climbed as high as was humanly possible in that tree, and hoped that would be adequate refuge. The bear was very powerful and tenacious, though. He began swatting at the tree trunk with his enormously strong paws. The Frisco Kid figured for sure that he was doomed. But, thankfully, the bear took too long in trying to knock the tree down, which allowed for The Frisco Kid's father to regain his consciousness. The Frisco Kid's father knew he had to protect and save his boy. The only thing he could think of was to try and fight the bear off. The Frisco Kid watched from the treetop as his father charged the bear with a severed branch from an Aspen tree. The branch came to a point at the end. The bear was too concerned with the boy to notice the father coming up from behind him. He stuck the makeshift spear right into the bear's right paw; the same one he was using to try and knock the tree down with. The Frisco Kid's father had heard somewhere before that the most painful place to strike a bear was in his paw. Apparently, he heard correctly, because the bear gave up after that, and actually ran off whimpering.

When The Frisco Kid told me this story, I didn't much believe it. I mean what bear runs away whimpering? However, that didn't take away from the fact that the story was entertaining, especially the way he told it.

We sat in that motel room conversing and tying one on. I had all but forgotten about Johnny, and the disloyalty he showed me earlier in the night...until he came back in the motel room with two girls. He was surprised to find someone else beside myself in the room. I believe he wasn't just surprised, but pleased about it. Johnny instantly took to The Frisco Kid, and The Frisco Kid instantly took to Johnny. One of the girls Johnny had brought along with him instantly took to the kid also. I was thoroughly upset.

I was tipped over the edge when Johnny basically told me to get lost, just not in those exact words. I remember it was something like, 'Hey Emerson, Pal, I saw a bunch of people hanging around in the lobby of that hotel down the block, why don't you go over there and check it out?'

Then, The Frisco Kid added, 'I think some of my friends are over there. We had a dance tonight.'

Everyone had erupted with laughter after that was said. I was mortified. But, instead of standing up to Johnny and voicing my own opinion, like any dignified human being would do, I just did what he told me. I took it, because I feared that if I did not, Johnny would not want to be my friend anymore.

It was an awful ordeal. I cried in the snow by that wagon wheel all night and into the morning. Damn it! I used to let Johnny walk all over me. I wished I had understood why.

I lit another cigarette and ordered another drink to divert my thoughts away from Johnny. I needed to do something; I didn't want to listen to Ella, and I definitely did not want to listen to my thoughts about Johnny. When Jane came back over with my drink I had to ask her a question, because just lighting a cigarette and ordering another drink did not sufficiently distract my thoughts. The first thing that came to mind was, "Have I done something wrong to you, Jane?" I didn't desire to ask that. I was not confrontational. Johnny was confrontational, and I hated Johnny right now. I certainly didn't want to be acting like him.

Jane looked over at Ella. Then, she looked back at me dryly, very dryly. "All I'm going to say is friends treat each other better than this...that's all I'm going to say."

She turned and walked away. I watched her all the way behind the bar. Why did she respect Johnny so damn much?

Ella didn't give much thought to Jane and her comment; she knew it was directed to me about Johnny. Jane can go to hell just like the rest of them!

Ella continued babbling. Much to my dismay, she managed to capture my attention just when I thought she might close her lips up for good. "Emerson? Emerson? Are you listening to me? Did you hear what I said?"

"What?" I literally had no clue as to what she had been talking about, or what she might have been referring to.

"Johnny dropped out of school. He is going to pursue boxing for good. 'The Aussie' and Percy got him a once in a lifetime opportunity in Vegas next week. They managed to land him his first real bout. And it's against an actual contender. This is not some questionable tournament with nobodies; this is the real deal. Apparently, the contender is over the hill or something, and he is trying to make a comeback. 'The Aussie' dealt convincingly enough to line Johnny up as this contender's first fight back on his comeback tour. Johnny stands to make a good amount of money...not as much as the contender, obviously, but a good enough amount to get his career started. 'The Aussie' said that this was the only chance like this that would ever come along...that a shot like this rarely happens, if ever. Johnny Bea is a no name for heaven's sake! But, if by some stroke of God he happens to beat this guy, then it no doubt would put him on the map in the world of boxing...even if it were just temporarily. Which it probably would not be...you know how good Johnny is."

Amazing, just amazing. A little more than three months ago Johnny was nothing more than an aimless street fighter, a bully in the eyes of some, not knowing what he was going to do with his life. Now, obviously, he had it all figured out. Now he had a girl and a job! Just amazing. That stuff only happened to Johnny. Amazing!

"Both 'The Aussie' and Percy say that they have never seen pure, raw ability like Johnny's before. They say that he is already prepared for this guy. All they want him to do is train on his technique a little this week, but other than that they think he is ready." Ella concluded with a smile.

I was repulsed.

"Has he accepted?"

Ella nodded her head proudly. "He's at the gym as we speak."

"Great. Just great. Good for him. He deserves all of this. If anybody deserves all of this, it's Johnny Bea."

Ella could see the contempt in my eyes. "Come on, Emerson. I came here to patch things up with you and I and Johnny the best way I know how. Now, he and I are trying to get over this ordeal…this torment…and we're hoping you will try to put it behind you as well…"

"What about all that stuff Johnny said earlier…all that 'I'm going to finish this once and for all' talk? That was no more than a few hours ago, Ella!"

"We were fighting, about you, before you knocked on the door. And he was still upset with you. But I calmed him down…that was one of my stipulations…"

"What was one of your stipulations?"

She looked at me awkwardly and then reached into her purse. "I told him, flat out, that if he wanted to be with me then he would have to try make amends with you."

"I don't see him here!" I had never been so disturbed in my life. I knew something was coming.

"No, that's true, you don't. But I do have this." She pulled a white envelope out of her purse. She handed it over to me. I swiped it out of her hand with fury. What were these two trying to do to me? I didn't want this.

"There's a letter inside, from Johnny. He told me to give it to you."

"He knows you are here with me?"

She nodded. "Yes."

"What does it say?"

"I don't know, it's for you. But I believe it's Johnny's way of saying he's sorry."

"Yeah right." I stuck the envelope inside my jacket pocket.

"Maybe you should consider doing the same."

Who did she think she was? She was making it sound like she was completely faultless and blameless in this whole twisted affair...and yes, twisted is exactly what it was.

I laughed at her. She just shook her head and prepared to leave. "Well Emerson, I've done about all I can do, and I've said about all I can say. If it's not good enough for you, then I'm sorry, truly, but that is something you and your conscience are going to have to deal with...alone. Good-bye."

She started to make her way out the door.

I was blindsided by the harsh reality of the situation. Up until this point, everything seemed surreal...almost like a misguided dream. The truth of everything struck me right in the face, and it was inconceivably overwhelming. I turned around in my seat and caught Ella before she made it out the door. "So that's it?"

She nodded her head.

"Why?"

"Because I'm going with him, Emerson. We'll both be gone from this town, most likely for good, on Friday."

I closed my eyes tightly...so tight they hurt. "Just like that, huh?"

She nodded her head. "Just like that."

I turned back around in the booth. I couldn't bear to look at her any longer. I couldn't bear to look at her ever again. It was hopeless. I was hopeless.

Before the door to The Hill shut behind Ella, she said one last thing. "It doesn't have to be like this, Emerson…read the letter. You'll see. We could all be close again."

I waved my hand in disgust. "Go away."

I continued to defile myself the rest of the day until I passed out. Jane must have taken me back to my apartment, because when I came back to consciousness that's where I was. I was lying on my bed. I had all my clothes on, except my jacket. I got up to try and find my jacket. It was in the study room. It was slung across the back of my desk chair. The white envelope was sticking halfway out of the pocket. I retrieved it and took a seat in the chair. Before I opened the envelope, I looked over at the bottom desk drawer.

I suffered from heartache more than a headache.

Chapter 25

The paper smelled of tobacco as I pulled it out of the white envelope and opened it up. It read: *To Emerson Parks, My Friend. Love is a strange and powerful thing, Emerson. Up until now, I never realized the magnitude of that power. I was not ready for it. I was not capable of comprehending it. That is, until the trip to New York. I now understand. The strange part of love is that it makes you do stupid things. Things you would never do if you just were capable of comprehending the simple notion that you were 'In Love.' The powerful part of love is that it gives you the ability to forgive the stupid things that one does when they do not realize, yet, that they are in love.*

Love was at work this past weekend, Emerson, and it made every player involved do stupid things. And what did we learn from it? We learned that we are all in love with one another, in separate, unique ways. Ella made me realize that this is what was at work, and that this is what made everybody do what they did; this is what made me kiss that waitress at the bar that night; this is what forced Ella to sleep with you; this is what made you stick me in the side with that broken whiskey bottle.

You love both of us, Emerson. I see that now. It's not just Ella that you love...

I was beginning to sweat. I had to pause not only to wipe my face, but also to shake my head in disbelief. This could not really be how Johnny saw things? Was it so simple that he could blame it on an ideal? The ideal of love. The arrogance he displayed was boggling to the senses. I begged to differ. He was obviously intentionally misconstruing events, and leaving a few key parts out. So far, it was sounding to me like love was to blame, and certainly not him or Ella. It did, however, also sound to me like I was to blame, if love was not. My sweating intensified as indecent rage crept up my spine. I continued reading.

Love makes people do crazy things, Emerson. But that's okay. I love Ella with all my heart. Thanks in part to you, I see that now. Also, thanks in part to you, she sees that now too.

He was patronizing me, the son-of-a-bitch! I kicked the bottom desk drawer with fury, and it opened up halfway from the force. I noticed the orange shoebox within. I didn't feel much like closing the drawer back up this time.

I am willing to forgive both Ella and you, Emerson. I am willing to lay down my pride, for the principle of love, and apologize to you, Emerson. I am sorry, for doing what I did to your face.

What kind of apology was this? I kicked the drawer again. This time, the force closed it back up. I kind of liked having it open.

I know Ella has told you about everything, because she instructed me to write you this letter before she saw you. A lot of things have transpired in the course of the past couple weeks, my friend, but one thing I would like to remain constant: our friendship. I know things will never quite be the same as they were before, and to a certain extent that is quite regrettable...

Regrettable? Why? Because you always had the upper hand? You vindictive, pompous Son-of-a-bitch! You're not apologizing to me here. You're slapping me in the face again, only this time it's with your emotional vengeance, not your physical. Very sly, Johnny...very sly. Unfortunately for you, this time it's not going to work.

But the future is bright, Emerson, and I would be lying if I didn't say I would like to see you in mine. I hope you will understand and accept this gracious apology. The only way I will know for sure, if you do accept, is if you make it to my first professional boxing match this Friday in Las Vegas. I've got a seat reserved for you. Please come. It doesn't have to end with New York. Please come. Your friend, Johnny.

All I could do was laugh. I must have laughed for ten minutes straight.

I'll be there all right.

Chapter 26

I had never been to Las Vegas before. My father wasn't prone to risking the money he had earned all month long on a roll of the dice or the turn of a card. My mother was a Wayne Newton fan, but that was not a convincing enough argument for my father. When I was back in grade school, I believe it was seventh grade, the whole class partook in a field trip to this make-believe city called Exotic City. It was a fascinating idea, actually. The proprietor rented one of the floors of this old office building and turned each room on the floor into an educational, yet captivating place or location. I remember one room was the Serengeti and there were all these models and sculptures of lions and elephants and cheetahs and impalas. Another room consisted of the South American Rainforest, with colorful birds, unusual plant-life, and a permanent mist falling from the sky, or ceiling. The only other room I remember was the one that held a casino, supposedly set in Monte Carlo; I couldn't remember the educational facet of the room, but it sure enthralled my imagination. That was the closest I had ever been to a casino.

As I walked through the heavy glass doors I was

Drift

immediately hit with excruciatingly irritating sounds and colors. They were so irritating that it was mandatory that I go straight to the bar and get a drink. On the walk to the bar I realized the reasoning behind the horrendous colors and designs on the carpets and ceilings; it was so you would focus your attention on what was in the middle, between the carpets and ceilings. However, I found all the gaming machines with all their bells and whistles just as annoying. Even the people playing all of those casino games, of which there was a tremendous mass of, were a cause of unneeded aggravation.

When I arrived in the barroom, I was slightly relieved that the enclosed space muted some of the sound bellowing out of the casino hall. I shook my head as I took a seat at the bar.

The bartender wore a tuxedo, void of the jacket. His sleeves were rolled up and he had big round glasses on. He promptly threw a white cocktail napkin down in front of me and said, "First time to Vegas?"

I smiled. "That obvious, huh?"

He smiled back. "What can I get you to drink?"

"How about a screwdriver? And go easy on the orange juice, would you please?"

He laughed. "It's already affected you that bad, huh?"

"No, no. I'm just a fool for vodka…amongst other drinks."

"I hear you…loud and clear." He went off to fix the drink.

When he arrived back he asked, "Have you ever known a singular person…anyone throughout your whole lifetime that you might have met…who was a native of Las Vegas?"

I thought about it. I thought about it hard. I could not answer the man. "I'm not sure, but I don't think so. However, I might not be a good person to pose that question to…I haven't many friends."

"What? What are you talking about? Good-looking, seemingly intelligent, guy like you? No way. You've probably got people lining up to be your friend.

Now, take me on the other hand…you see this name here?" He displayed a black nametag on his vest. White lettering was embossed on it. It read: Lance.

"Lance. Yeah, so that's your name."

The bartender shook his head. "No it's not. My real name is Arnie…Arnie Mack. Not Arnold Mack like a normal person would be named…but Arnie Mack. Can you believe that? I think my parents named me after some cartoon character, or something like that."

"So."

"So! So, my friend! So I've been teased virtually my whole life because of my name…I guess when you combine that with my look I'm an easy target for ridicule."

"No way, you're joking? You seem like a regular old guy to me."

"Your kind, but you don't need to say that."

"I'm not just saying that, I'm serious. If you were picked upon for some reason when you were younger about the way you looked, then in my eyes you have grown out of it. And, as far as your name is concerned…well that's your name. You don't want to change that, right?" I took a drink and then added, "I guess you already have, though…too late."

The bartender smiled. "Actually, I haven't…not for good at least. You see, I'm a nobody. I always have been. I came to Las Vegas to be a nobody amongst nobody's. In this town, a nobody can be somebody, because everybody is a nobody. That's the beauty of it. That's the allure. That my friend, beings me back to my question. No one ever seems to stabilize here…why? Because we're all a bunch of nobody's!"

"So you chose to become Lance The Bartender, instead of Arnie The Sufferer?"

"Exactly. I'm Lance the Bartender…I'm somebody."

He smiled and walked off to go help another customer who had just made her way up to the bar. I looked down at her. At that time, I noticed we were the only two patrons in there.

She was ostentatious in her beauty…supremely confident. And she should have been, she was the most attractive woman I had ever seen. She was even more attractive than Ella. I wondered if I would have thought that a week ago. I took another drink and sized her up. She was much too striking for a normal guy…that was plain to see.

The bartender made his way back towards me after he took her drink order. He noticed I was eyeing the goddess. "Just another nobody, my friend. Just another nobody."

I looked at him seriously. He looked down at her. I looked over.

Sensuously, the goddess pulled out a cigarette and lit it. She stared at me out of the tops of her eyes the whole time as she did so. I wasn't quite sure what to think. Perplexingly, my heart (or at least my loin) was not racing for her. She was much too gorgeous for someone like me. But, even with that realization, I still should have lusted for her. But I didn't.

I took another drink to thwart the headache I felt coming on. The bartender was fixing the goddess her drink right in front of where I was sitting.

He continued speaking to me, "I just met you no more than five minutes ago, but I can sense it about you…"

"Sense what?"

"I think you belong here, with the rest of us."

I looked at him scornfully. He laughed and then walked off to deliver the drink to the goddess.

When he came back I said, "What exactly do you mean by that?"

"I see a lot of people come in here my friend…an awful lot. But there are very few in which I see myself in their eyes. Sure, your exterior is elegant, but man, you're lost on the inside."

I couldn't believe the transformation from affability to audacity that took place in this bartender…and in only a few short minutes. Moments ago, he said I probably had friends lined up waiting for me to accept them, or something like that. "What was all that stuff you said earlier, my friend? Huh?"

"I spoke to soon…much to soon. I see now that you belong out here in the land of nobody's."

I threw down a five-dollar bill, only enough to pay for the drink, in sheer disgust. He didn't deserve a goddamn tip. "Have a nice life, Arnie."

I retreated to one of the booths in the lounge. Lance the Bartender laughed the whole time it took me to find my seat in the lounge. I shook my head in disbelief. What was this world coming to?

I took another drink and picked up a local newspaper that was lying on a table in front of me. I flipped through it until I found the Sports section. In the lower left-hand corner of the front page there was an announcement about Johnny Bea's boxing match. It was a big announcement. I couldn't believe it. The fight was in twenty minutes from now. I planned on finishing my drink and then making my way to the arena.

I took another drink and threw the newspaper back down on the table. I was feeling heinously horrible. When I looked up, the goddess was standing in front of me. She was almost as tall as the ceiling…so it looked from my vantage point. Her dark hair glistened in the soft light from above. She wore a glamorous, but sexy, black strapless dress that hugged every curve in her body...she had curves I had never seen before.

I couldn't understand why I felt indifferent about her.

"Do you mind if I join you?" Her tongue was delicate, yet assured.

I shook my head.

She asked me what I was drinking, and then ordered another round from the pestilent bartender before she sat down. She sat directly to my right, as close as she could possibly get without touching me.

When Lance the Bartender brought the drinks over he acted as if he had never seen me before. I laughed him off while the goddess stared at me. I was extremely uncomfortable, but I tried not to move a muscle. I took a quick drink.

The goddess asked, "What's your name?"

"Emerson."

"That's a nice name…a strong name."

"It is?"

"Sure it is. I can tell you are a strong person."

"Yeah? How so?"

"Just by looking at you."

"Your bartender friend didn't seem to think so."

"Who? Lance? I don't get it."

I felt like the two were in on some clever ruse together, and I was trying to be played the fool. "Forget it." I said plainly, and then lit a cigarette of my own.

"What are you doing here, Emerson?"

"Just having a drink."

"No, I mean in Vegas. What are you doing in Las Vegas?"

"I'm going to the boxing match being held here in a couple of minutes."

"Why would you want to do a thing like that?"

I chuckled underneath my breath. "That's a very good question. I asked myself that numerous times on the drive down here…numerous times."

"You drove here?"

"Yes."

"From where?"

"Denver."

"You must be dog tired."

I nodded my head.

"Why would you want to go see a couple of goons lug it out when you could have a stupendously good time with me?"

I wasn't sure if she was trying to sound funny, but she did. I shook my head and shrugged my shoulders. I felt like saying I don't know, but I didn't.

"You're strong, Emerson, but you're a lover not a fighter…that is easy to figure out."

"Is it now?"

She smiled and then extended her left hand. Her fingers were as long as snakes. She placed her hand on my thigh and gradually ran her fingers up and down it. I did not feel an ounce of sexual desire anywhere in my body for this exceedingly attractive woman. I knew I should have, but I just didn't.

What was wrong with me? This was the prettiest lady I had ever seen.

"Why don't you forget the fight and come upstairs with me? I guarantee you a better time."

I finished off my drink. "Let's go."

I was beyond confused.

As we walked out of the bar I added, "All that I ask is that we put the fight on the television when we get up to your room."

"Sure, no problem."

When we arrived in the room, the first thing she did was turn on the television for me. She found the channel the fight was on and turned the volume up. There was pre-bout commentary going on, which I was definitely not interested in. However, it was more appealing to me than this beautiful woman…who was now beginning to unzip her dress. She sure moved awfully fast.

"Here, Emerson, can you help me with this? I always have trouble."

I walked over to her. My eyes remained on the television. I took them away from it for a moment to focus on the dress. I unzipped the dress. It slipped off of her long and sleek body. She wore nothing underneath.

I stared at her in hopes that her beautifully exposed body would get my blood flowing, but all it did was make me more upset. I rapidly turned away and walked back to the edge of the bed. I sat down and found the television again.

Johnny was making his entrance into the arena. He looked good…real good. He looked healthy and refreshed…ready to take on the world. I knew he was going to.

"What's the matter, Emerson? Is that stupid, pointless fight more entertaining than me?"

The goddess started to dance, right in front of my face. I tried to look away, back towards the television, but she blocked my view.

"I think this was a bad idea. All I want to do is watch this fight, really."

"Nonsense."

She straddled me, and then went for my pants. Her persistence was unbearable. I heard the ring announcer introducing the fighters.

"Honestly, I don't think this is going to work."

"Come on, Emerson, just relax and go with the flow."

The bell to signal the opening round rang.

I tried to jostle and position my head to see the fight, but she was too lengthy and she had leverage on me. I had no other choice but to pick her up and throw her off of me.

At that same moment, the contender fell hard to the canvas. Johnny had knocked his opponent out cold in the first thirty seconds of the opening bout commencing his professional boxing career.

I dropped my head in my hands and started to weep.

"Hey, what's your problem Mister? You must have something wrong with you." The goddess said furiously as she gathered up her dress from the floor and slid it back on.

"Get the hell out of here!"

I was relieved she demanded my exit. I had to get out of there. I had to get out of the casino. I had to get out of Las Vegas. I had to get out of this world I was wrapped up in.

No longer could I hear myself think. My senses went dull, entirely dull. I felt nothing.

I found my car and jumped in the driver's side. The orange shoebox occupied the passenger's side. It was begging me to open it up. I lifted the lid and removed it. I looked inside.

Just then, like a bolt of lightning thrown at me from the heavens above, I was struck with an overwhelming sense of direction and purpose. Somehow, someway, I knew what I had to do.

There was a payphone directly next to where my car was parked. I got out of my car and dropped my coin into the slot. I picked up the phone and dialed Jackie Blasé's number.

When she answered I said, "Jackie, I think I want to hear the rest of that story you started to tell me."

It was then that I realized there were no worlds, and that all one can do is Drift through life in hopes of creating one of his own someday.

The End.

Printed in the United States
5877